A DANGEROUS
RETURN

T0154585

OTHER BOOKS BY RIQUE JOHNSON

Love & Justice

Whispers from a Troubled Heart

Every Woman's Man

A DANGEROUS
RETURN

RIQUE JOHNSON

STREBOR BOOKS

NEW YORK LONDON TORONTO SYDNEY

Strebor Books
P.O. Box 6505
Largo, MD 20792
http://www.streborbooks.com

This book is a work of fiction. Names, characters, places and incidents are products of the author's imagination or are used fictitiously. Any resemblance to actual events or locales or persons, living or dead, is entirely coincidental.

© 2007 by Rique Johnson

All rights reserved. No part of this book may be reproduced in any form or by any means whatsoever. For information address Strebor Books, P.O. Box 6505, Largo, MD 20792.

ISBN-13 978-1-59309-043-2
ISBN-10   1-59309-043-9
LCCN 2006938904

Cover design: © www.mariondesigns.com

First Strebor Books trade paperback edition May 2007

10 9 8 7 6 5 4 3 2 1

Manufactured in the United States of America

For information regarding special discounts for bulk purchases, please contact Simon & Schuster Special Sales at 1-800-456-6798 or business@simonandschuster.com

ACKNOWLEDGMENTS

First and foremost I'd like to acknowledge the talent and the blessing that GOD gave me to share with his children. I pray that I remain worthy of the gift.

To my fans; you have no idea what your continued support means. It means that you have embraced and found some substance in my words. It means that you have identified with a character in one of my novels. It means that you have felt like you were present in a particular scene in my books. It means that you've felt an emotional outrage because of my words or have had your juices run rampant with an excited sensation. It means that your imagination has been taken places beyond reality. It means that I must remain worthy of my blessing and to you...wherever you are. Many thanks and continued blessings to you.

PROLOGUE

Jason fulfilled his promise of taking his soul mate to dinner and later returned home for their chosen dessert selection, each other. Afterward, Monique lay with her head on his chest comforted by the simple but alluring embrace. She held her hand out in front of her, seemingly admiring a make-believe ring. Jason broke her comfort, sat up and gazed into her eyes, somewhat caught between a thought and a hard place. Monique glared back, identified his expression as one of concern.

"What is it, Jason?"

"I want you to have something, but first I need to know if you'd accept it."

"It, as in?"

"It's best if I show you."

Jason excused himself, walked to the closet and returned with a medium-sized box. He rambled through its contents, found and handed Monique a diamond solitaire, two-plus carats in size.

"What is this?" Monique asked barely able to contain her excitement.

"It's yours if you'd accept it."

"Why wouldn't I?"

"It belonged to Sasha."

Monique looked into his eyes. She saw such emotion in them that she took time to reflect on the knowledge of his relationship with Sasha.

"Jason," Monique said carefully, "if my memory serves me correctly, you once told me that it was the memory of Sasha who helped you love me."

"Something like that. As strange as it sounds, Sasha spoke to me some way, somehow. I received whispers from a troubled heart, my troubled heart, and her spirit showed me all that I needed. She lifted the pain that I was feeling and released me to love you."

"With this in mind, I'd be honored to wear this symbol of your love. I don't want you to ever forget what she meant to you. I'm indebted to her, we both are."

At that moment, Jason realized that this and more amazing times were in store for him. He took the ring from her hand, placed it on her finger, and then politely kissed her on the lips. The simple act caused Monique to blush.

"Excuse me," she said in an excited state. "I could definitely get used to this."

For the next few moments, they coexisted in silence. Monique was curled comfortably in his embrace. They seemingly had blocked out the television that played in the background until the words "twenty-eight days for twenty-eight million" awakened their consciousness. They left their solitude and directed their attention to what the newscaster was saying. When the segment ended, they shook their heads in awe.

"I know that the person who bought that ticket is feeling sick," Monique said.

"Probably not, Dear...it seems to me that if someone has twenty-eight days left to claim twenty-eight million dollars, then it stands to reason that this person either lost it or does not realize that he or she has the winning lottery ticket in their possession."

"That makes sense. I can see myself doing that. Sometimes I can't remember my words, much less remember to check a lotto ticket."

"Say that again."

"I'm saying that I often forget to check my ticket after a drawing."

"No, you said, remember my words."

"And?"

Jason didn't respond. He basically stared through her as he attempted to recall why those words were so familiar to him. Out of the blue, his subconscious mind blurted, "Sasha."

"What about her?" Monique asked.

"Who?" Jason responded after snapping back to reality.

"You called Sasha's name."

"Did I?" Jason asked rather dumbfounded. "It was Sasha who said those words to me that night I proposed to you."

"What are you talking about?"

"It's a long story. Remember my words," Jason recited again as he sat on the side of the bed. "Remember my words. She must have been referring to her journals."

It became clear to him, clearer than the brilliant VS-rated diamond Monique was wearing. His mind bounced to a bookmark located in one of her journals and he recalled thinking how strange that a lotto ticket would be used for such a purpose. Jason reached into the box of Sasha's possessions and blindly began removing the journals in search of what was calling him. He placed each gingerly on the bed as if they were delicate glass.

On the fourth try, it felt right. It was right; a small block of paper was extending from the journal's pages. Jason held the journal up to Monique's eyes.

Without even looking, Jason said, "This is it."

"Jason, truly I'm lost," Monique confessed.

"That piece of paper," Jason announced as his eyes focused on it, "is worth twenty-eight million dollars."

"No way, things like that don't happen to ordinary people like us."

"Your statement is flawed. We are extraordinary people. Take it."

Monique found what Jason was saying well beyond belief, yet, somehow his conviction to his statement, the sentiment it carried, made his words all too real. Her heart raced as she plucked the paper from the pages.

"The prize amount is?" Jason asked.

Monique flipped the ticket over, cut her eyes from Jason to it, back to Jason. Suddenly her mouth became dry. She swallowed before she spoke.

"Twenty-eight million," she replied with a cracked voice.

Jason stood, smiled and walked into his home office. In a few seconds he was browsing through Virginia's Lottery page. Monique was too nervous to walk. Even sitting down, her knees trembled as she anticipated the outcome.

"Angel," Jason called, "Come in here, please."

"Honey, I can't, just tell me."

Jason stood in the doorway. "Well, it appears that we have a newfound fortune."

Monique's mouth opened without a sound. She gazed at Jason in disbelief, seemingly discarding his words. Jason allowed Monique to gather her composure before he sat next to her. Immediately, her arms held him in a strong, silent embrace.

"This is," Jason spoke calmly, "quite a turn of events considering my poor upbringing."

"Remember, I knew you back then, things weren't that bad for you."

"You're looking at it from the outside because things weren't good at all. I remember one Christmas my mother wanted to get me something to wear and something to play with, but money was tight. So, she bought me a pair of pants and cut the pockets out."

Monique's face dove into confusion. She stared at him, followed the gaze with a smile and then a burst of laughter.

"That was silly," Monique said.

"Silly enough to make you laugh."

"Here I thought we were having a serious conversation, somehow, again you manage to add humor."

"We needed something to break the tension."

"It's strange, seems to me that we would be overjoyed with the money, but we're acting differently."

"Believe me...inside there is a fireworks display grander than the Fourth of July celebration at the Washington Monument. I guess everything surrounding how we became wealthy is mind-boggling."

"So," she said smiling, "what are you going to do with your free time?"

"I've always wanted to learn how to play golf."

ONE

Monique bathed in the hot sun topless. This piece of paradise was the last stop on their vacationing tour before returning to Virginia City. They had spent two weeks respectively in Aruba, Barbados, Saint Thomas, Bermuda and concluded their extended vacation in Puerto Rico. She and Jason lay on beach towels tanning their bodies that had beads of sweat rolling down their oiled skin. They in-dulged themselves on the bow of a rented yacht that ironically was named "Monique's Pleasure," anchored in the Caribbean Sea. It was a one hundred-ten-foot yacht that had every amenity imaginable. They had sailed to a secluded cove off the main Puerto Rican island for their own private sanctuary on the water.

"Honey, does it get any better than this?" Monique asked with her eyes closed.

"Nothing can be better than quality time with the one you love," Jason responded.

Monique turned her eyes away from the sun, toward Jason and opened them slowly as if he were a Christmas present that she hardly believed she had received.

"I love you too...even before the riches, but I can't complain about being spoiled beyond my wildest dreams."

"Yes, early retirement never felt so good. Are you ready to get back to the real world?"

"Semi."

"Yes, life as we knew it will be different when we get back."

"Waking at home at our leisure will be a wonderful thing."

Jason opened his eyes, turned his head toward her and discovered Monique in a heavenly gaze.

"Why such a passionate look?" Jason asked.

"I don't know. I think it's the magic of the moment combined with how the sun's rays are tantalizing my nipples," Monique confessed.

"Oh?"

"It's like my body's warmth is being charged from the heat coming through my nipples."

"Do you want to take another dip in the water to cool off?"

"No, I'm okay. The heat makes me feel rather nasty."

"Nasty good or nasty bad?"

Monique smiled. Jason sat up, reached to his left and filled his glass with more Mimosa. He took two decent-sized swallows, followed by a huge one, then fell to his knees and lowered his lips onto one of her nipples. *They are hot*, Jason thought.

"That's refreshing," Monique responded.

"Think it will help you cool off?" Jason asked.

Before Monique could respond, Jason used his tongue to swirl a piece of ice around her hardened nipple.

"Yes, but your method warms me in delightful ways," Monique panted.

Jason switched to the other nipple and probed it until the remaining ice dissolved.

"What do you think you're doing, Mister?" Monique asked excited by Jason's actions.

"I'm cooling you off," Jason teased.

"Not like that you aren't."

"Okay, okay. Have more Mimosa."

"Thank you...nasty person."

Monique picked up her empty glass, leaned back on the towel and rested on one elbow as she extended the glass for a refill of the satisfying beverage. The cold drink that met her flesh felt even colder because the raging sun baked her skin oven-hot. Monique screamed. She believed that her man had lost his ever-loving mind. She sat up quickly, momentarily overtaken by the sudden chill that invaded her skin. Jason moved the cold liquid stream from her stomach and poured onto her hidden desire, where Monique now experienced two uniquely different forms of wetness.

He tilted the pitcher upside-down; the ice cubes tumbled down like tiny glaciers crashing onto her tightened stomach muscles. Jason lifted her bikini bottom fabric and placed two rectangular ice cubes under the garment. He strategically placed one cube against her lower lips and made sure that the bikini bottom held it in place. Monique screamed from the excitement and pleasure of Jason's playfulness.

"I don't believe you," Monique announced. "What if I did you like this someday?"

"That would be fun, but not today. Today my only mission is to serve you."

"Jason," Monique moaned as his lips closed over the ice cube through the garment.

The ice was like liquid hydrogen on her as it would be on a man, thus a means to prolong her orgasm. Monique's clitoris popped up as if the tune for the Jack-in-the-Box had just ended. Jason sucked on the ice cube for a long while as he alternated the pinching of Monique's nipples. This prompted the cube to move to Monique's toy surprise.

"I feel like it's going to pop off," Monique moaned in deep passion.

"What does?" Jason asked as he paused to nibble on her inner thigh.

Monique refused to solidify Jason's rhetorical question. She couldn't answer if she wanted to; she was too far gone to formulate a reasonable answer. Jason's mouth was heaven to Monique's passion and the pleasure pain received from the alternating nipple pinches, all but helped Monique lose her mind. The ice yielded to the constant warmth of Jason's mouth and Monique's increased body temperature. Jason sensed by the feel of it on his tongue that her clitoris had softened and his soft warm tongue had produced greater, sultrier battle cries from Monique.

Jason didn't know if it was the gentle rocking of the yacht, the ultraviolet rays that constantly bathed her skin, or his wondrous instrument, but he couldn't remember a time when Monique's hips had bucked so wildly. He slid a finger between her pleasure haven and the garment, curled his finger and pulled it to the side, then dove back into her flesh with his hungry mouth. Oddly, the strangest thought materialized in his mind, *Now that's old school*.

Monique's passionate moans were more sensual and erotic than he had ever known. Like a computer building a microchip, Jason danced his tongue around, in and out of her womanhood in a poetic fashion. It was lyrical. These lyrics performed as a current and ignited the electrical circuitry that took information back to her orgasmic processor. Monique suddenly slapped both hands on the bow, rose to a sitting position and watched Jason perform his magic. The visual of her being pleased provided the last piece of information Monique's processor needed. Monique bellowed in a gigantic climax that started with the words, "Damn you, Jason" and ended with a descent in volume series of "Oh, oh, oh's."

Monique pushed away from him at the shoulders to escape Jason's overbearing mouth. Jason wiped most of the natural juices from his face on Monique's inner thigh, and then finished the rest with a portion of the beach towel.

"Had enough?" Jason joked.

"Man, if you don't get that weapon from me, I'll scream."

"My weapon as in…?"

"Dangerous," Monique interrupted. "That tongue of yours. Honey, I'm too sensitive, you need to allow a girl time to regain composure?" Monique asked with a demand disguised as a question.

"Not a problem."

Jason excused himself, returned with two more dry oversized towels and placed them in an area near Monique.

"So what are you going to do with those?" Monique asked after noticing that Jason was still aroused.

"Well," Jason replied. "This particular weapon will disengage once I lie back down and relax."

"I see," Monique commented playfully. "One of us once stated that a hard-on was a terrible thing to waste."

"Would that one of us happen to be you?"

"I don't remember," she lied.

Monique kneeled next to Jason, placed both hands at his waist and pulled at his swim trunks.

"What are you doing, Ms. Sensitive?"

"Trying not to be wasteful."

"You're so bad."

"Actually my love, this is going to be good...now raise your damn hips," Monique stated forcefully.

"Yes Ma'am," Jason stated.

After the garment was removed, Monique took a note from Jason.

"We're going to tan him for a moment," Monique stated before she dashed away with the empty pitcher.

In the short time that Monique was gone, Jason found himself enjoying the sunrays on his manhood. He touched it as if he was checking to see if it had cooked sufficiently. *Interesting*, he thought.

No sooner than the thought faded from his memory, Monique's hand squeezed his tool as if she was extracting gel from a tube. The move startled him partly because his eyes were closed while he listened to the waves splashing against the yacht, but mostly because Monique's hand was cold. Prior to her seizing Jason's tool, her hand was submerged in the pitcher with water and ice.

Monique placed her other hand in the cold water and simultaneously lowered her mouth onto him. She did this before her previously chilled hand had time to warm completely. Her hot sensual mouth elevated Jason's erotic state. He closed his eyes and felt the sun's rays try to penetrate through his eyelids. Monique had been in her position far too many times for Jason to remember, but this time, her mouth felt as soothing as the first taste of warm apple pie.

She gauged Jason's mounting excitement by the slow movement of his hips. Suddenly Monique stopped and gave him a taste of the first sensation by stroking him with the cold hand from the bucket. Another adrenaline rush consumed Jason, but when she placed a couple of ice cubes against his genitals, Jason would swear that his blood had frozen. The warmth of her mouth teased him again. Jason bathed in the sensation that was almost heavenly. He was speechless and completely inundated by her spell. The movement of a soft pleasing tongue coupled with chilled genitals couldn't be put into words. Monique continued the hot-cold treatment until her hands couldn't withstand another dunk into the freezing water. Then, she spent a long time showing great patience enjoying her throbbing tool. Jason, on the other hand, had subdued his release for the past few minutes. If he relaxed, an explosion grander than the bomb dropped on Hiroshima would occur.

"What do you want?" Monique asked in a sultry voice.

Jason didn't respond to her inquiry. She asked the question again, immediately after her mouth left his hardness.

"I want..." Jason panted, but continued to hold his orgasm.

Monique stood tall above him, removed the hindering clothing and straddled her joy backward in the reverse cowboy maneuver. Her cushiony haven accepted Jason slowly, willingly and uninhibited. Her hands were at the side for support as if Jason's manliness had penetrated too deeply for that position.

Jason pulled one of her arms behind her back, then the other. Monique gasped as her body fully accepted him. She wanted to scream, but she remained motionless in order to adjust to the pleasure pressure that filled her. Jason used his pinky fingernail to trace an imaginary line from between her shoulder blades, down to the center of the small of Monique's back. Monique responded with a small hip movement. Jason retraced the line once more and a similar response came from Monique. Jason traced the same line so many times that a red trail became visible on her sun-baked skin. It burned to touch, yet it aided in the sensation that Jason's manhood was giving her. However, during the process, Monique's hip movements had quickened and become a rhythmic motion that she wasn't aware of.

She wanted to buck wildly through the orgasm that swept her. Instead she oddly leaned forward and was awed that Jason's manliness extended deeper into her. She squeezed her internal muscles hard for a count of three before releasing and executing the move again. Her reward was a series of "mini-gasms," her word for the quick ending yet pleasing orgasms. Monique noted that with each squeeze of her muscles, Jason's tool throbbed uncontrollably. Moments after she held and released the last of her mini-ones, Jason's juices filled her, perfectly timed as though their act had been rehearsed one thousand times. Jason moaned pleasurably. His passion cry was different than most. It was filled with more exuberance and delight. Jason's wondrous sounds thrilled Monique's ears.

Monique wasn't finished. She squeezed, held it tight and slowly lifted as if she was removing him from within her. She released the muscle control just as Jason was exiting her, and then slammed herself back down deeply onto his tool. She squeezed, held the muscle control tight and began to lift her body from him.

"Uncle," Jason announced as he slapped her butt with one of his hands.

"What was that?" Monique chuckled. "You're quitting?" she asked almost in laughter.

"Just for the moment," Jason panted.

Their bodies were sweaty, aided by the sun that seemed all their own, but primarily from the secretions of the act itself. She was pleased; her man was pleased. All was good. She lay backward, her back against his hairy chest and felt a sting from the trail that Jason made on her back. Yet, she marveled in the sensation of their union as Jason's arms draped around her in a soothing embrace.

"Could it be that the Jason Jerrard was vocal when he came?" Monique joked.

Jason smiled before replying, "Not me, never."

"Today, my Dear, you were loud. I loved it."

The rebuttal concerning the amount of noise Jason had made continued for a small moment and concluded with Monique stating to Jason that she and the fish knew the real truth. They lay connected in the embrace for what seemed like hours, each being satisfied with the solitude.

TWO

A few hours later, Jason docked the yacht at one of the smaller islands located off the northeastern tip of Puerto Rico's mainland. It was a private pier located near the location of Jason and Monique's sexual excursion. The dry land destination was a restaurant called The Cove where he, Monique and the younger Jason were to dine.

The Cove previously was a cave that had been transformed into an upscale restaurant. The restaurant itself was a risky move for the investors, primarily because there was no electricity or running water on the tiny island. Yet, the vision came to life by building a miniature power plant that supplied electricity for it and the pier that welcomed the guests. Piping water to the island proved to be the biggest challenge, but with the time and a well drawn-out plan, the impossible became possible.

Inside the restaurant the ventilation system was exposed much like ventilation systems in log cabin homes. Lights hung from above in all six of the eating areas, a result of strategic drilling. The seventh area was the kitchen. Special rock mass sonar equipment was used to determine the best routes for ventilation for the ovens and other cooking apparatus. There was a main area where the general public ate. The other five areas ranged from quaint and intimate to a medium party size. The furnishings were all handcrafted with intricate native island details.

Jason's rented yacht was docked at the pier for private boat owners. The general public arrived every thirty minutes by a ferry that shuttled patrons to and from the main island.

Jason and Monique had changed into semi-formal wear and were sipping on fruity drinks in a coconut shell, compliments of the restaurant when the younger Jason approached them holding the same drink.

"This place is pretty impressive," Monique's son spoke as he gave his mother a hug.

With Jason's warped sense of humor he yelled out, "Group Hug," seconds before his arms draped both of them. The three of them laughed. However, Monique's laughter was a disguise to conceal the joy she experienced having both of her men engulf her.

"How long have you been waiting for us?" Monique asked her son.

"Not too long...just long enough to have started my second drink," he answered while holding the coconut in the air.

"They are refreshing," the older Jason responded.

"Especially mine, it's...what's your word again?" the junior Jason asked the senior. Before Jason could respond, the word "leaded" sprung from the younger one's mouth.

"You have coffee in your fruity drink?" Jason joked.

"Not exactly. The lead in my case is called banana rum."

"Now I see why you're so happy," Monique responded.

"Mom, I read you like a book and you know it. So tell me, why are you glowing? What did you two do on the water all day?" her son joked.

"We...ah," Monique stuttered too embarrassed to comment. "Grown-folk stuff that's none of your business," she replied with a flushed face.

Her son smiled brightly and commented, "Even though you look like the cat that ate the canary, I won't pry further. Having a sexual undertone discussion with my mom isn't my idea of comfortable conversation. And the visuals," he continued, left the rest in the balance. The three burst into simultaneous laughter.

At Jason's request, they were seated in the second smallest eating area. It was just large enough to comfortably seat four people and serve them full-course meals without them having to rub elbows. Beyond the magnificence of a cave transformed into an upscale restaurant, Monique and Jason received joy from the apparent attraction between her son and the female waitress that served them. Jason took the tease further and switched seats with his junior so that she could be watched without having to look over his shoulder.

The waitress introduced herself as Caramel. She gave each of them an equal amount of eye contact during the welcome speech and talk about the daily specials. However, when her eyes met the younger Jason's, there was a bashful smile, followed by an apparent blush, the result of Jason's playful wink. She asked for the drink order without breaking the glance between them and walked away with a little more pep in her step.

"It looks like one of us has a definite admirer," Monique joked.

"More like, an admiration between the two of them," Jason commented.

"She is striking," the younger Jason said in his defense.

"Pop quiz," Jason stated. "What do you like the most about her?"

The younger Jason displayed a smile that only a man whose hormones had been affected would understand.

"Besides that." Jason laughed.

"Everything. I feel something warm coming from her. A sense of 'I need to know her' is present. However, the dark brown bedroom eyes, lovely smile and other physical attributes don't hurt either."

Monique was amazed with their conversation and was even more proud of her son. Throughout the years, he had always dated attractive women. Caramel was no exception. The difference with her was that she was heavier than the rest, definitely out of his norm. Though she had a larger frame, she remained proportionally built and still very shapely. Monique was happy that her son could look beyond the superficial physical appearance and discover the person within. Well, at least she hoped that to be true and prayed that he wasn't looking for a quick night with a native.

When Caramel returned with the drinks, Jason flashed another bright smile and the effect on her was nervousness. This was indicated by the slight shake in her hands as she placed the drinks on the table. Oddly enough, Monique remembered that she was like that eons ago when she first met her Jason.

"So, have you all decided on what you'd like to eat?" Caramel asked.

Jason motioned for Monique to speak first; afterward, the younger Jason insisted on the senior to order next.

"And you, Sir?" Caramel asked Monique's son. "Have you decided?"

"Please call me Jason," he replied.

"Okay, Mr. Jason, what would you like?"

"Take this down," Jason junior recited in a devilish tone. "Seven...Zero...Three...Five...Five...Five...Seven...Two...Nine...Three."

Caramel wrote Jason's home telephone number down and waited for him to continue.

"Other than that," Jason continued, "I'll have whatever you think is good."

"Are you sure?"

"Yes, surprise me."

Caramel nodded and walked away.

"Who does that remind you of?" Monique asked her fiancé.

"I would do something like that, wouldn't I," Jason responded, followed by an all-knowing smile.

"I figured," the younger Jason commented. "When she didn't refuse my number, she wouldn't lead me wrong with a meal. What?" Jason asked defensively when he noticed his parents grinning at him.

Moments later, Jason's and Monique's food was placed in front of them respectively. Each plate had a mountain-piled-high main entrée and other side items. Caramel's idea for the younger Jason's meal was a saucer plate with a lone piece of toast on it. Jason, his mom and Jason stared at the bread oddly.

"This is considered a five-star restaurant?" Jason asked of his flirt mate.

"It is," Caramel replied. "I assure you, we are five-star in all aspects."

"And, this is the best that you can offer me?" he asked with a slight hint of disappointment.

"No, on the contrary, all of the food here is grand," she answered evenly.

"Then the toast represents?"

Caramel smiled, she knew that she had stunned him. "It's simply the surprise that you asked for," she responded. "It represents you not destroying your appetite because as you can see, the portions here are grand. How could we have dinner tonight if you've eaten already?"

"Tonight?" Jason asked. He looked back and forth between his parents. "I get off in an hour...interested?"

Jason nodded, smiled and spoke, "It would be my pleasure, but I have to be on the last ferry to the mainland."

"Then, our date could start on the way back on the ferry because that's my ride too."

"Sounds like a plan," Jason confirmed.

Caramel nodded and her date watched her walk away in awe. Of course, for the remainder of the threesome's time together, Monique and Jason teased him relentlessly.

THREE

The weather was unusually warm for early spring; it was downright hot and too damn humid according to Kaylyn Croft. She rode down Route 7 in Tysons Corner, Virginia headed for Jared. She was a sultry woman, model height, taller than most with a Chinese bob hairstyle that all but accented her hazel green eyes. She was feeling mighty special as she rode to her destination in a Mercedes 500 SL convertible with the top down.

Kaylyn arrived at Jared fifteen minutes early for her appointment. Jared was an exclusive jewelry store chain in the Washington, D.C. metropolitan area. The common consumer didn't have the luxury of just walking into the store and shopping. They served customers by appointment only. Jared's offered the finest quality jewelry and the most brilliant diamonds on the East Coast. The store had metal detectors at the lone entrance. Armed guards patrolled outside of the building and were strategically placed inside. One would wonder if Fort Knox had as much protection.

On the top of Kaylyn's shopping list was a three-carat, marquise-cut diamond stone that she had been waiting to arrive at the store. She was prepared. She had drawn on a piece of paper the type of setting that she wanted for the precious jewel in advance, confident that she'd like it.

"Good afternoon," the security guard stated. "Your name and appointment time, please."

He was familiar with Kaylyn because of her other appointments, but since the surveillance cameras watched the entrance, he proceeded with the formalities.

"It's at one-thirty."

He tapped a few buttons on his clipboard-sized PDA, verified her appointment, then stepped aside and allowed her to proceed to the security checkpoint. Inside, Mike Miller, Kaylyn's salesperson, held up his hand to get her attention. He was a well-dressed man who reaped the rewards of being the store's top salesperson.

"I'll be right with you," he stated. "I'm finishing up now."

Kaylyn nodded. The salesman's current customer was Sebastian Cole, the Lieutenant Governor of Virginia. He had been reported as being the youngest governor in Virginia's history. His tall frame towered over Kaylyn's by at least six inches. Mike and Sebastian shook hands and Sebastian turned around abruptly not knowing that Kaylyn was directly behind him.

"Whoa," he announced just inches away from invading her space. "I'm sorry," he continued. I should not be in such a rush."

"No apology needed. I may have been standing too close behind you."

"Still, I need to be more observant...Mike," Sebastian addressed. "Take care of this lovely lady. She deserves a good discount for me almost wiping her out."

"I always look out for my best customers," Mike responded.

"Again," Sebastian said to Kaylyn, "my apologies, have a wonderful afternoon."

"Thank you, have a great day yourself."

"That's a very polite fellow," Kaylyn said to Mike.

"He is indeed. You and he became customers about the same time. You don't know who he is, do you?"

"No, should I?"

"He is only the youngest Lieutenant Governor in the history of this state."

"That's Sebastian Cole...he looks totally different on TV. You never know who you are going to run into these days."

"So true. Are you ready to view what I have for you to choose from?"

"I'm dying with anticipation. Show me! Show me!" Kaylyn recited overjoyed.

Mike showed Kaylyn two stones that were nearly identical to the untrained eye. But, to Kaylyn's trained eye, the slightly smaller one had more clarity. So, she chose the two-point-eight-nine-sized stone over the three-point-two-sized stone. Mike wasn't surprised that she picked clarity over size. Most people who know their gems do. She gave him the paper that had the creative design setting for her selected stone and was assured that designing it would not be a problem. Kaylyn was to return in a week to pick up the finished product.

The first thing that Kaylyn did when she stepped out of the jewelry store was to put on her designer sunglasses. Her head turned toward the sound of a car door closing. She looked over the rim of the shades and saw Sebastian approaching her.

See, I was going to leave you alone, Kaylyn thought.

"Excuse me, Ms.," Sebastian stated. "I'm Sebastian..."

"Sebastian Cole," Kaylyn broke in.

"So, you do recognize me?"

"I do now; Mike just told me who you are."

"I see...I hate to be forward, but you are so striking that I couldn't leave without a formal introduction."

"Thank you. It's a pleasure meeting you, Governor."

"Lieutenant Governor."

"Still, I've never met anyone in the political arena before. I'm honored."

"Don't be, I'm a regular guy, you'll see...that's if I can appear charming enough to sway you to go out with me."

"Don't you politicians have security and bodyguards?"

"Well, for the Governor and up, that sort of thing is twenty-four-seven. I have to request protection and it's nothing compared to what they get."

Kaylyn wrote her name and number on a piece of paper from her purse. "Call me sometime," she stated as she handed him the folded piece of paper.

"I'll surely do that. Any particular day that you're free?"

"My schedule varies, so surprise me."

"Hum," Sebastian contemplated her suggestion. "Okay, how about a brunch or early cocktail, right now?"

"Now?"

"Yes, if your afternoon is free."

Kaylyn leaned against her car, and again peered over the rim of her glasses. "You're serious, aren't you?" she asked.

"As serious as I can get without being offensive. What harm can it do? You can even pick the place."

"I don't know why I'm even considering this. I don't like being in the public eye."

"It will not be as bad as you've perceived it to be. Look around," Sebastian said with his arms spread wide. "Is there a media frenzy now? People don't recognize me, just as you didn't recognize me. How about it?" he asked, then playfully poked his bottom lip out as if he were pouting.

"Very well. We have to be brief. I have an appointment later."

"Thank you. I'll only take up a moment of your time. Today that is," he relayed, and then smiled devilishly.

There was something about the playful smile that relaxed Kaylyn. She did, however, hope that his charm wouldn't be too addictive because she really didn't want to get drawn into him.

Kaylyn and Sebastian started their afternoon together at the new nightspot called H2O. It was a short drive away, located at the marina just off the Potomac River in Washington, D.C. It had been redesigned and modernized since it had changed ownership and renamed from Hogates. H20 still possessed a dinner area where one could get some of the finest seafood dishes in the entire Washington, D.C. metro area. The dance floor was smaller with the redesign to accommodate an additional bar. In short, H2O wasn't considered truly upscale, but being the newest place in town, it commanded a lot of attention.

Sebastian and Kaylyn sat on a loveseat that gave them a view of the water. Several moderate to expensive-looking yachts were docked. In particular there was one that outshined the others.

"Welcome to H2O," the waitress said as she placed cocktail napkins in front of them. "What can I get for you today?"

"Good afternoon, Keki," Sebastian commented after reading her nametag.

Keki was a woman about four feet nine inches with auburn hair that was rolled and pinned in a bun.

"Do your parents know where you are?" Sebastian joked.

"I know," Keki said after smiling. "I have a young-looking face and yes, I'm old enough to serve you drinks. I hear the same thing every day. What can I get you folks?"

Kaylyn ordered the house red wine and Sebastian ordered a frozen margarita with no salt.

"So, Lieutenant Governor, what is it about me that makes you ask a perfect stranger out for drinks?"

A lustful smile slowly occupied his face. "I don't have a colorful answer to that question, but I can tell you that I had a strong sense...better yet, you struck me as someone that I should get to know."

Kaylyn looked at him long and hard while she digested Sebastian's comment.

"Really? You know," Kaylyn joked. "I could be the black widow spider."

"You don't look like the type that would kill prey after you've loved them."

"Maybe you'll just get your heart broken."

Sebastian squinted his eyes before he asked, "You don't pull any punches, do you?"

"All that I'm trying to say is, maybe it will prove unwise to get involved with me."

Kaylyn's words entered his ears. Sebastian acknowledged and accepted the challenge to proceed with caution. That was until his male ego took over. Miraculously her words became distorted, twisted into something his pride could accept.

"I'm going to make you love me," his ego boldly spoke before he flashed another devilish smile.

"What?" Kaylyn expressed. "You are confident of yourself," she stated because of his grin.

"Did I say something wrong?"

"I suppose you spoke a truth that related to your abilities, but I want to believe that your spirit is far better than that."

An equally devilish smile was returned. After their drinks were placed on the table a second and third time, Sebastian's words and mannerisms became induced by the alcohol and seduced by Kaylyn's outward beauty.

"How about continuing this party at my place?" Sebastian suggested flirtatiously.

"Don't you think that you're getting ahead of yourself?"

"I think you and I are feeling pretty much the same thing. You've had your own outright flirtatious moments too."

"That's absurd! I believe that you've had too much to drink. But, if we continue, it will be at my place."

"Is that a yes?"

"Is that questioning a concurrence to my suggestion?"

"To enter or not to enter the spider's web?" Sebastian joked.

Kaylyn smiled back. She had resisted his advances, but her own internal question was, "do I work or do I not work?" knowing that Sebastian's persistence could prove detrimental to him.

When Sebastian entered Kaylyn's townhouse, he was impressed with its size. The thirty-seven-hundred-square-foot dwelling was larger than some single-family homes, but an extra like the elevator that traveled between the first and third floors made it unique. Sebastian hadn't yet discovered what she did for a living, but he was awed with the layout of her home. It was as though they had the same taste.

"I like this," Sebastian complimented. "Truly, I do."

"Thank you. A girl tries."

Kaylyn directed him into the living room where the neo design, though tastefully done, struck him as odd compared to the other areas of her home.

"This is my favorite room in the entire house," Kaylyn commented. "Everywhere in the room is like viewing an abstract painting."

"I agree. It's very picturesque. So, where were we before leaving H2O?" Sebastian seductively asked.

"I thought that the drive over may have calmed you down some."

"Trust me, the effect that you have on me is not entirely a direct result of the alcohol I drank. You're simply stunning."

Kaylyn blushed before bringing her eyes to his. "Thank you," she said.

Sebastian returned a passionate gaze. All of him wanted to pounce on her. Kaylyn's body called him like no other before.

"We shouldn't do this," Kaylyn softly spoke. "Our sleeping together hours after just meeting you seems..." Kaylyn paused as she searched for words that would let him down easy.

"Seems like two adults are sexually attracted to each other," Sebastian interrupted. "Am I wrong for speaking for both of us?"

Kaylyn's head shook from side to side.

"Then, is there anything wrong with consenting adults enjoying each other's company as long as we practice safe sex?"

"You don't want to get involved with me," Kaylyn warned.

Sebastian stood for no other reason than to hug her, but when Kaylyn's second warning acknowledged in his mind, a puzzled look accompanied the words, "Why wouldn't I want to be involved with someone like you?"

"I'm a complicated woman," Kaylyn stated with her eyes focused on the floor.

"Meaning?"

"Meaning, I just am. Have you ever heard of the expression, all that glitters isn't gold?"

"Yes, a time or two."

"Then, that's me."

"Complications for me are when I'm noticed with any woman. All of a sudden, I'm painted as the most eligible in Virginia has a new love interest."

"You're an attractive man. Early indications with me dictate that you are well grounded. Your being in the political arena would surely have its benefits, but trust me when I say, I'm not the woman for you."

The third warning got Sebastian's full attention. For the first time her words sunk in.

"Okay," Sebastian stated rather defeated. "I'm putting my pre-notions aside and will acknowledge that you're trying to tell me something. So, what exactly am I being given words of caution about?"

Kaylyn looked in his direction. Actually she was staring through him in search of the truth, partial truth or anything that would ease both of their minds.

"I wish," Kaylyn confessed, "that I could tell you about me, but as life would have it, I just can't."

"Things with you can't be that bad. Look at what you've accomplished. It would appear that you have a wonderful lifestyle. Things can't be that bad."

Kaylyn stood in front of Sebastian with her arms draped around him in a tender hug. She held the embrace for an extended period in silence. As her arms released the warm comfort of his body, she stated, "I think you should leave now."

Kaylyn's words were a direct contradiction to the way the hug made him feel but, somewhere buried within, there was a sentiment that he couldn't ignore.

"May I at least leave my contact information? I'd really like to hear from you again."

"I don't know. A later time isn't going to make it easier for me to allow you to get to know me."

Sebastian's mild disappointment was apparent on his face. A thousand words of rebuttal ran through him, yet he politely nodded.

"Understood," he stated as he pulled car keys from his pocket. "Thank you for the time that you've allowed me," he continued. "It has been a pleasure meeting you."

"And, it has been my honor meeting you, Lieutenant Governor."

Sebastian gave her a polite kiss on the cheek, turned and left her home without uttering another word. Kaylyn watched his proud, but disappointed steps leave the confinement of her home with a great deal of sadness. As she slowly walked to secure the dead-bolt lock on the front door, she briefly smiled upon seeing Sebastian's card sitting on the table at the door.

"Some men ask for trouble," she said aloud before picking up the card.

FOUR

Late evening, a couple of days after their enchanting evening at The Cave restaurant, Jason and Monique entered their Northern Virginia home in Virginia City. Their extended vacation had ended; yet they felt as though a vacation was needed to rest from their vacation. Then again, both being retired, they had plenty of time to rest. Jason dropped the bags at the front door and Monique tossed her purse onto the loveseat.

"Care for a nightcap to wind down?" Monique asked.

"Indeed...one of those wonderful apple martinis you make, please."

"Coming right up."

"I'll be right back," Jason said. "There is something I want you to read."

"More poetry?" Monique asked.

"You know me well. It's something I wrote before we went on vacation. It's a reflection of how I felt a day or so after we met in high school."

"What made you reminisce back that far?"

"Don't know, give me a second," Jason said as he walked toward the bedroom. When he returned, Monique placed two drinks on the coffee table and sat next to Jason on the sofa. They made a toast and sipped their drinks before Monique picked up the single sheet of paper that Jason had placed on the coffee table. The poem was entitled "Someone." Monique read:

Sometimes you meet someone and their aura changes you for all eternity.
Sometimes you know that this someone bestowed on you, with all intents
and purposes is sent to confuse you, yet is yours forever.
Sometimes you wonder if this someone recognized the magic moment...

that quick blink of an eye when an insignificant minute's moment
becomes significant.
What happens then? Do souls unite or hearts intertwine, mending as one?
Do we someones live, breathe together, draw our strength and life substance
from the very thought?
To holding our hearts hostage, destined together.

"I like this," Monique confessed. "It shows a deeper side of you."

"Thank you. I often think about our beginning."

"So, are you going to tell me what your magic moment was?"

"That's easy. Do you remember when you chased me into the room where we changed skates?"

"I do."

"What did you do to me in there?"

"I kissed you for the first time."

"That was my magic moment. Tit for tat?" Jason asked.

"Surely, my magic moment was the first time I laid eyes on you. Although, I never meant to confuse you."

"The confusing part was your pursuit of me because I was almost three years younger."

"Well, we're here now and my magic moment continues today."

Monique lay across the seat and placed her head comfortably in Jason's lap. Jason rubbed her forehead tenderly, concluded the caress with his fingers running through her hair. The stroke was soft, caring and soothing to Monique.

"Honey, maybe you shouldn't do that because I'll surely fall asleep," Monique said.

"I'm tired too...who knew that an extended vacation could be so exhausting?"

"We have been on a constant go for well over a month. It's only natural. So, what's on the agenda for tomorrow?"

Jason looked down at Monique's closed eyes and stated, "To continue to wake naturally. After that, who knows maybe? Go play a round of golf. Play at it, at least."

Monique knew her man too well and knew that his last comment was a result of the frustration of his "I can master anything" attitude.

"You've just started playing. Your game will come around," she stated comfortingly. "Just don't be on the course during your retirement ceremony."

"That's this week? I forgot all about it."

"It's on Friday, my dear."

"I'm being used as a pawn once again."

Because of Jason's good fortune, he was able to take advantage of his belief about retirement. He believed that retirement was a monetary issue and not necessarily related to age. His and Monique's fortitude of having Sasha's winning lotto had netted them just over fourteen million after taxes. It had allowed him to retire at the ripe old age of forty-six and Monique at the age of forty-eight.

Jason's retirement seemed to come at the right time. Even though his previous efforts stopped a brutal killer and relieved Virginia City of the tedious killings, he wasn't entirely in the clear because of the Mayor's wife's involvement. Crystin, the Mayor's wife, had a full recovery from the injuries inflicted by Dakota. But, with Captain North, the DA and the Police Commissioner counting each expansion of his chest, more than ever he felt that he was being set up to fail. He had always conducted his detective duties on the edge, but his familiar position had converted into a much too delicate balancing act. One that he felt would hinder any future accomplishment as a police official. Therefore, as he had often said, his riches came right on time.

The good part about it was that his police work spoke for itself. His questionable antics that brought him criticism also made him the most successful detective in Virginia City. He also held the record for arrests, convictions and solved cases by one individual in the entire state of Virginia. When Captain North received Jason's resignation letter, the word flew up the chain of command like electricity to a light bulb. It invoked the Commissioner to twist the Mayor's arm to have a public retirement ceremony for Jason. Behind the ceremony, the Mayor hoped that it would shed a positive light on the people of Virginia City's psyche and downplay the ever increasing crime rate.

The ceremony was held on a Friday afternoon. All of the pieces of the puzzle had gelled like epoxy on a fine piece of china. Two high school bands provided entertainment and as an added bonus, they were to have a battle between them as if they were rival college bands. Balloons, cotton candy and other festivities added a lighter side to the occasion.

The similarities between this ceremony and the previous one that Jason had the pleasure of attending made him feel a bit uneasy. Especially since the seating arrangements had the Mayor's wife, Crystin and Monique sitting next to each other. Jason noted the unfriendly glare between them. Crystin's expression while she glanced at Jason contained disgust for him and the fact that Monique was Jason's woman, a greater degree of that sentiment carried on to Monique. Simply put, Crystin was pissed.

Although her emotions for Jason had lessened, these same emotions had left a bitter taste in her mouth, a bitter taste of pain. It was as if Jason's presence lingered inside of her for no other reason than to cause despair.

Monique's attitude more or less stated, "He is my man now, BACK OFF!" Monique couldn't recall a time when she felt so defensive about a man. But, it wasn't just any man; it was her precious high school sweetheart, Jason Jerrard. She felt the hairs on her neck stand at attention just being near Crystin. Somehow Monique felt that Crystin would not make it through the event without putting her foot in her mouth. Monique had foreseen the future. Remnants of the thought were still on electrical impulses throughout her brain when Crystin said something under her breath.

"What was that?" Monique asked back.

"I said," Crystin spoke a little clearer, "be careful, he is going to use you too."

Monique's head moved side-to-side truly rejecting Crystin's notion.

"Not my Jason," Monique spoke proudly.

The tear that ripped through Crystin's heart could almost be heard by the others sitting within ear range on the stage. She felt like crying, but refused to give Monique the satisfaction of knowing that she had been emotionally moved. Crystin's eyes began to swell with tears. She closed them for a long period of time, seemingly in a self-induced sleep. Without any warning Crystin sprang from her seat and briskly walked to the stretch limo next to the stage. This, however, was after she surprisingly slapped Monique in the face with an open hand. Monique was too astonished to respond. Her mouth fell open; she held her face where Crystin had slapped it and began a small circular motion to bring blood back to the area. As Crystin made her way down the short flight of steps, the reality of the situation fell upon Monique.

Oh no the bitch didn't! Monique bellowed inside.

She attempted to follow Crystin, but Jason placed his comforting hand onto hers and held her in place. His fingertips teased the back of her hand as means to indicate that they would deal with the matter later. Monique looked in Jason's eyes and spoke, "If this wasn't your day," very softly.

"I understand," Jason responded back in the same manner.

The Mayor also witnessed his wife's actions. He was surprised; yet he understood Crystin's pain that brought on her aggression. He possessed his own pain for the direct betrayal that Jason inflicted on his trust. However, the politician in him forced his personal feelings aside. He continued performance in an attempt to charm the patrons with his wit. At the conclusion of his speech, the Mayor introduced Captain North who gave the audience a detailed account of Jason's career at the Sixteenth Precinct. He focused on the young officer Jason Jerrard and told how he knew Jason would be unique and troublesome the very first day on the job.

He talked of how Jason had replaced him as a hostage when a captive broke free and had unexpectedly started choking him from behind with a nightstick that he wrestled from an officer.

"There I was," Captain North stated, "gasping for breath. I told all of the officers to put down their weapons. They all complied except Jason. Jason in his rookie wisdom started a dialogue with the man and convinced him that he wouldn't escape with a night-stick alone." Captain North paused, looked back at Jason, and continued with his recount of Jason's actions. "Imagine my surprise when he offered the man his pistol. Jason's condition to the assailant for the weapon was that he replaced me as the hostage.

"The assailant locked his forearm around my neck to free up one hand to accept Jason's pistol. He then pointed the gun at me and asked me to walk away slowly when Jason was about two feet away. I can still vividly remember seeing Jason's hands go up as he asked that everyone remain calm. Jason winked at me as we crossed paths. With a gun, the assailant felt assured that he now had the upper hand, and he began making demands for a safe passage out of the state. Jason suggested to him that ground transportation would be too risky, therefore, he instructed me..." Captain North paused. "Mind you, he had known me for a mere few minutes...to arrange for a helicopter for the man to escape.

"Jason spoke so many outrageous demands for the gunman, all intended to feed on the gunman's power trip. He had the criminal gloating over a false victory to where he had not noticed that Jason had placed his hand in his jacket pocket. When the criminal regained consciousness, his hands were handcuffed behind his back. He was lying face down on the floor with his senses not completely intact. In his groggy state, he noticed another officer and I assist Jason to a sitting position in his spot on the floor. Jason's conscious mind came back to life when Sgt. Austin broke a smelling capsule under Jason's nose.

"I asked Jason why would he place himself in danger..."

Jason stood from his seat and yelled to the audience, "I saw an opportunity and took advantage of it." He sat back down as the crowd began to chuckle.

"He is being modest," Captain North said. "I vividly recall him saying to me in no certain terms that a ship without his Captain navigates blindly. So, you all get an idea of how he started out being a maverick from the very beginning."

"What method did he use to free you?" A yelled question came from the audience.

"Oh, that. He used a taser and knocked himself out cold when he triggered the hidden device in his pocket. Jason's body acted as a conduit and carried the electrical shock to the gunman, seriously stunning him.

"Right then, I knew that I'd have my hands full with his antics and through the years, he didn't let me down. I covered his butt so many times; I started putting him down as a dependent on my taxes."

After a minor laugh wave filtered through the audience, Captain North introduced Jason. He stood at the podium overlooking the audience. His speech was delayed as he pondered his own internal question, "Is this the end?" The question played in his mind like a never-ending chorus of a song. As he attempted to gather his thoughts, he scanned the citizens of Virginia City almost like they were his own children. He was proud to have protected and served them. He started his farewell speech by commenting on the part of the story that Captain North had omitted.

"By the way," Jason said as he turned toward Captain North. "You failed to tell the people that the gun that I gave the criminal had no bullets."

The Captain and all of the parties sitting on the stage simply shook their heads from side to side. Jason's real speech started with, "I've always dreamed of being a policeman." The emotional speech ended several minutes later with, "It has been my honor to have been your loyal servant. Thank you and God bless."

When the Mayor switched places with Jason, he had to actually beg the applause to stop so that he could get the band competition underway. After all of the festivities had ended and the majority of the patrons had gone, Captain North, the Mayor, Crystin, Jason and Monique were standing near the rear steps of the stage.

The three men were engaged in a cordial conversation while Monique stood behind Jason simmering like a stew. Though the sting of Crystin's slap had long left her face, Monique's pride kept a tingling sensation present. This was the catalyst of Monique's raging emotions. It was also the reason why she tapped Jason on his shoulder.

"Hold these," Monique demanded of Jason with her hand already extended to give him something. Monique walked over to Crystin who watched her with complete defiance and disgust.

"Mrs. Mayor, may I have a quick conversation with you?" Monique asked.

"I believe that I've said all that I need to say to you," Crystin commented rudely.

"In that case, I'll be brief," responded Monique.

Monique's fist connected with Crystin's eye swiftly and unexpectedly. She had thrown the punch with so much anger that she wasn't sure where it might land. She leaned over Crystin who was knocked to the grass, looked at her knuckles, and then wiped Crystin's eye juice from them with a portion of Crystin's garment.

"I believe that I've concluded our conversation, you think?" Monique boasted.

The men darted to the rescue of their respective women. Jason pulled Monique away while the Mayor sat up his bruised-ego wife.

"I want to press charges against that bitch!" Crystin yelled. "You all saw what happened."

"Are you okay?" the Mayor asked.

"I'm fine other than a burning sensation in my eye," Crystin replied somewhat shaken.

"We should get you home because your eye is starting to swell."

"No!" Crystin snapped. "Not before I press charges against the prissy bitch. You all are my witnesses," she bellowed loud enough for everyone to hear.

"Yes, we witnessed Monique's aggression," Captain North said. "And, we also witnessed your aggression against her earlier on the stage. So, why don't we call it a draw and get on with our lives. After today, I see no reason why your paths should cross again. How about it?"

Crystin was about to announce her rejection to the Captain's suggestion, but the Mayor interrupted and agreed with Captain North. Crystin's mouth dropped, she was astonished by her husband's comment. Her eyes bore through her spouse. She imagined thousands of sharp knives flying into Jason's body and pictured Monique's head in the cut of a guillotine. Her imagination went beyond that, she saw Monique's severed head lying in a woven basket and wished that it were true so that she could spit on it.

"You've got to be fucking kidding!" Crystin yelled at her spouse.

"No, I'm not," the Mayor responded firmly. "We both need to put Jason out of our lives. You see where his heart is; let him go as I've done with this retirement ceremony."

"He hurt me," Crystin spoke without realizing that she'd verbalized an internal thought.

"You aren't alone. His betrayal hurt me too," the Mayor responded.

The Mayor shot an appalled, disgusted expression at Jason. It was a signal to say he was through with the city's Boy Wonder.

"I'll repeat this statement for a third time," the Mayor continued. "I think that I've said all that is needed."

By this time the Mayor had helped Crystin to her feet. He nodded to the Captain before he and his distraught Mrs. crawled into the limo, then quickly drove away. As the vehicle made its way to the main road, Captain North was the first to speak.

"So, what have we learned today?" Jason's ex-boss asked.

Jason smiled at Captain North, and then gave Monique a larger brighter one.

"I've learned that my bride-to-be is compassionate even when she is angry," Jason commented.

"That Muhammad Ali left hook she threw showed no signs of compassion," Captain North replied.

"Oh yes it did," Jason countered as he opened his hand with the item that Monique had given him. "Imagine Crystin's condition if Monique's punch had been thrown with this ring on."

Sasha's engagement ring had been replaced and moved to Monique's right hand. Monique's new engagement ring picked out just for her was bigger and grander. It had a two-carat, raised-center, princess-cut stone with baguettes descending from the middle of the large stone to the band and decent-sized diamonds encased on the sides of the band. Captain North's eyes widened as his mind conjured the possible injury with the ring on.

"It would have been virtually impossible to call it square had you struck her with that," Captain North spoke to Monique.

"Well," Monique commented back to Captain North, "do unto others...

and I know that I wouldn't want to be struck like that. Besides, being engaged to a detective, you learn a few things about the law."

"All I know," Jason chimed in, "is that you've shown me a side of you that I've never known."

"I wasn't going to drop to her level," Monique responded in her defense. "But, your comforting hand couldn't lessen the rage her actions placed in me. So, when an opportune moment came I responded. I bet she thought she had gotten away with striking me. However, I do apologize to you both for making a spectacle of myself."

"Seems to me, Jason is rubbing off on you," Captain North joked.

Jason and Monique both laughed at the Captain's implication of Jason's character being mimicked by Monique. Unknown to them both, Monique found the piece of humor as a compliment.

"Honey, you are through with this, aren't you?" Jason asked Monique.

"I'm good. I hold no grudge. Hell, you can invite her to our wedding." Monique stated with a straight face.

Jason shook his head with the underlying implication of what an invite to their wedding might bring.

FIVE

Jason and Monique returned home humored with Monique's description of how Crystin fell to the ground. Jason joked that Monique's aggressive behavior resembled Mike Tyson's. Monique relayed again to Jason that she had every right to strike back.

"Do unto others," Monique repeated to Jason.

"Sweetheart, just remind me never to get on your bad side."

"Don't worry; there will never be a need to strike you."

"I'd be a ducking fool," Jason joked.

"Besides, I'll forever remain a lady with you."

"Yeah, but your aggression against Crystin wasn't lady-like."

"Trust me. I was brought up to believe that once a woman raises her hand to strike a man, the being thought of as a lady shit goes out the window."

"Ah," Jason responded. "A wise tale. A very wise one indeed."

Monique simply looked at her man. Jason started a fresh pot of coffee, joined Monique in the living room and the two lovebirds cradled on the sofa. Monique marveled in Jason's embrace, closed her eyes and inhaled as if to take in his very essence. She opened her eyes and then raised a brow.

"Your girlfriend sent you a letter," Monique said.

"She wouldn't do that," Jason joked. "She knows that we have to be very careful with our affair."

"Please do, because I'm not one that looks for trouble and don't want to find it lying about."

"I know that about you...so, why the comment about a girlfriend?"

"Your girlfriend wants you to know that she sent you mail, so she sent you a letter in a pink envelope."

Jason's eyes focused on the end of the coffee table where he had dropped the mail.

"Does that look like it came from Cleveland?" Jason asked.

"Why Cleveland?"

"That's where my girlfriend lives," Jason joked.

"Fool."

Monique excused herself from Jason's embrace and picked up the colorful envelope, looked at it oddly and passed it to Jason. The envelope had no return address, nor did it have Jason's address. It simply had his last name written with large letters across the face. Jason then noticed that the envelope had not been sealed. The back flap was tucked inside. Jason unfolded the piece of paper the envelope contained and immediately felt a bit of tension.

"*ACT I – The Introduction, we're coming after you,*" was all the letter contained.

"What now?" Jason voiced his first thought.

"What's wrong," Monique asked, intrigued by Jason's tone.

"I haven't been here to piss anyone off, so why are people fucking with me now?"

Monique read the note and instantly understood why Jason's level of concern was high. It was as though the terror alert for her man had been elevated to Code Red.

"What are you going to do?" Monique asked.

"There isn't much that I can do, but wait and let life unfold. Whoever this person or persons are, they will eventually reveal themselves. In the meantime, I have to say that we're safe."

"How so?"

"I've seen your left hook," Jason joked.

"Dear, please don't take this too lightly. Someone took the time to put this in our mailbox; I'd have to say that they are serious and have malicious intentions."

"And so am I. I haven't thrown caution to the wind. Trust me, dear, this letter," Jason stated as he crushed the letter with his hands, "has my full attention."

Jason followed up the statement by making sure that all of the doors and windows were locked and secured, even though he knew that they already were. Jason wished that he had answers. For the first time he was clueless as to whom he may have pissed off. He fought hard to keep a straight face around Monique, but Jason was perplexed. He was very troubled and felt that the note left for him was an act of terrorism. Whoever had left the note had succeeded in adding a bit of fear in him. And, every bit of instinct advised him that Monique was very much frightened as well. The anticipation was the worst part. He felt something else; sensed something more disturbing was about to come down the pike. He worried about Monique's safety.

"Do you know what this means?" Jason asked Monique.

Monique determined by the sound of Jason's voice that she was about to find out. She simply looked at him and waited for him to continue.

"Those firearm lessons that you didn't want to take are a good thing now."

Monique glanced at the note that had been thrown back onto the coffee table, sighed heavily and stated, "I have to agree with you."

"That's very pleasing to hear. Care for a refresher session tomorrow?"

Monique only smiled. She knew that Jason had her best interests at heart. Ten fifty-three the next morning, Monique fired the first rounds from her new automatic pistol at the nearby indoor firing range. The thirty-two Llama was slightly larger, slightly heavier than the twenty-two automatic pistol that she was accustomed to. However, the added size of the bullets gave her a more secure sense. The feeling was almost like a person moving from a small car to a perceived overpowering SUV. She felt confident and in control.

The firing range was like a breath of fresh air to Jason. He used to routinely visit the range far more often than the once-a-month mandatory requirement dictated by the police policy. It was his first time there since a few months before his retirement, however, his skills remained keen as ever.

"Just like riding a bike," Jason announced to Monique.

She had just fired the last round from the twelve-clip magazine, removed the ear protection and asked Jason, "What was that?"

"I said shooting accurately is just like riding a bike, isn't it?"

"For you maybe. I haven't come here enough for the act to feel like second nature. However, this thirty-two has a much smoother release."

"Don't shortchange yourself. If you can tell the difference between triggers, then you are a more advanced shooter than you give yourself credit."

"Thank you, dear. One day I'll be just like you," she said as she released the magazine from the pistol and replaced it with a full one.

She and Jason replaced their ear protection. Monique took aim at a target a hundred meters away.

"Between the eyes," she stated as her finger slowly applied pressure to the trigger.

The four shots took about sixteen seconds to execute based on Monique's approximate three-second delay between each trigger pull.

"They felt like good shots," Monique said.

"I'm sure they were," Jason responded. "Now, I'd like you to try a strange exercise," Jason suggested.

He pushed a button to reel the thick paper target to the eighty-meter range. He stood behind her and lifted her arm toward the target.

"This time I want you to aim for the left arm," Jason said. "The trick is, after you take aim, close your eyes and hold your breath for ten seconds. Then pull the trigger at the ten-second mark."

Monique did as instructed; ten seconds after she closed her eyes, the pistol fired.

"How did that feel?" Jason asked.

"I don't believe I did that well. I sensed how unsteady my arm was. It surely moved away from the target."

"We will see when we bring the target in. Let's try it again though, use the right arm as your new target."

Jason stood behind her. Once she sighted the target's right arm, he supported her firing arm with his right hand at her elbow.

"Close your eyes," he said softly. "I'll count."

He heard Monique's breath release at the ten-second mark, then the pistol fired.

"How was that?" Jason asked again.

"I was more relaxed with you steadying my arm, but did you have to count so seductively?"

"You're nasty no matter what you do, aren't you?"

"Well, it's no secret that I like being touched by you in any way," Monique confessed.

Jason pushed a button to reel the target in. The closer it got, the more justified Monique's comments about the shots being good became. Her first four shots were in a straight vertical line. One centered in the forehead, another in the mouth, one in the neck and the last was center cut in the chest.

"I'm very impressed with your shooting," Jason told Monique.

"Then you should be impressed with your teaching ability."

"Thank you, but this target shows that you're a natural."

"Well, with my eyes open because I missed the left arm with them closed. Together we hit the right arm."

"Don't worry about it, it will come to you. The exercise was designed to steady your aim and at the same time develop a feel for shooting. You have a good feel already though. Now, there are two things that I should be wary about when it comes to you."

Monique knew that Jason was seconds away from saying something smart. Jason verbalized all that she believed. Her hands went defiantly to her hips in anticipation. "I'm fearful of your left hook and I know that I'll never want to be in your line of sight when there is a gun in your hand."

"You better recognize," Monique said, then followed the comment with ridiculous laughter.

SIX

Captain North had pretty much been a hermit and had hibernated since his wife had passed seven years ago. To avoid a prolonged mourning period, he poured himself into his work. He started spending countless hours at the station and often spent the night on the uncomfortable sofa. Rumor had it that shower stall number two belonged to him. He actually had many makings of home in his office and locker to include several changes of clothes. The other joke amidst in the air was he spent his life at work cleaning up Jason's messes. A rumor he constantly denied, although Jason's troubles kept him from dealing with his own issues. He reluctantly admitted to himself that he missed Jason's colorful reports and found that he hadn't used a highlighter pen on any report since Jason had retired. Those highlighted parts were portions that required his superiors' immediate attention.

It was late evening, just before ten. Captain North rubbed his tired eyes. He had finished reading the day's reports and was contemplating whether or not he'd just crash his tired body on the sofa again. He rolled back in his chair, placed his feet on the desk and smiled at first glance of his feet because he couldn't remember putting on his bedroom shoes.

"At least they aren't shower shoes," he chuckled aloud.

Captain North reflected on an earlier conversation between two of his officers and used the thought as if the brightest idea he'd ever had had hit him. He sprung from his seat, grabbed a fresh set of civilian clothes and headed for the shower. In a short while he sat at Jazzpers. It was a premiere jazz club located in Southwest Washington, D.C. The defunct movie theater located in L'Enfant Plaza had been transformed into one of the hottest places in town. His fingers were drumming and feet were tapping to the sound of live music.

All in all, he was feeling good about the night out. Eons had passed since he had stepped into any club, but quickly he realized that only the faces had changed. The male-female mating rituals were ever present. He watched one woman, probably many years his junior, sitting at a table for two with settings for both. A bucket of Dom was being chilled with one glass empty and hers half filled. Captain North acknowledged that she had been sitting alone for quite some time and deduced that the presence of another had kept the other watchful eyes from approaching her. Yet, the gorgeous woman's eyes peered at the entrance in search of someone.

Someone is very late, Captain North thought to himself.

He watched her finish the glass of expensive champagne, then pour herself another glass of liquid courage. He nodded as their eyes connected for a brief moment and turned his head quickly when her brilliant smile made him blush internally.

What would Jason do? the Captain oddly thought. *He'd probably think of something stupid to say to break the ice*, his thoughts continued. As if thoughts of Jason's antics were the mechanism for his sudden courage, he swallowed hard and approached the woman's table. Even though the woman was flustered with her date's tardiness, she presented him with a warm smile.

"Please excuse me, Ms.," Captain North stated. "You've been waiting for someone a long time."

"I am and he has pretty much pissed me off," her soft voice spoke.

"It's understandable. A woman as charming as you need not wait for any man."

She flashed her smile again. Captain North blushed again.

"May I offer to keep you company until he arrives?"

"That's very sweet of you, but I spoke the truth about being pissed."

"All the reason why I should join you. I'm hoping that I can make the time go by more pleasantly."

Captain North couldn't believe that he was being bold. He'd considered himself well out of the game, however, the rush of excitement with the act itself overwhelmed him. The woman glanced at the entrance once again, followed by a more disturbing look at her watch.

"Sure," she stated. "I'd welcome company at this point."

"My name is Frank North," he said as he began to sit. "It's a pleasure meeting you. I just figured that if he wasn't here now, he wasn't coming."

"I'm Daiquiri Drinks."

She noticed Frank's expression to be much like everyone else's when she told her name.

"And yes, that is my birth name and yes, my parents had a sense of humor," she added in advance of what would be his next two questions. "Thank you for being concerned about my being here alone. As you can see, I was waiting for an associate of mine who just made partner in our law firm. I suppose more important things came up."

"Did you at least receive a call?"

"It is apparent that you've watched me for a while, therefore, you would've heard that thing ring," she said with a nod directed at the cell phone sitting on the table.

"I suppose I would have."

Daiquiri Drinks was a woman who, absent the crow's feet around her eyes, showed no real signs of aging. She had short auburn hair and a body that rivaled women many years her junior.

"Shall we make a toast?" Daiquiri suggested. "Feel free to drink with me. After all, it's paid for."

"Thank you. You're too kind," Captain North said. He picked up the champagne glass. "What shall we toast to?"

Daiquiri raised her glass and didn't blink an eye when she toasted, "To assholes that don't know how to keep a date."

Captain North's facial expression didn't hide the fact that her toast threw him a little.

"And to saving gestures," Captain North said, concluding the toast.

"I do appreciate you not letting me wallow in self-pity. I promise you, I will not endure that state any longer. So," she smiled even more brightly, "Frank, may I call you that?"

"By all means, please do."

"How often do you come here?"

Captain North smiled rather bashfully. "Would you believe that this is my first time?"

At first, Daiquiri thought that she was being lied to, but the more intently she looked, she saw how frightened and unsure her new acquaintance was.

"I sense that you're telling the truth."

"Truly, I am. I thought that I'd do something different for a change, so I came here for a change of pace."

"What is your normal routine?"

"I work late most days. Being a Police Captain, I never seem to catch up on paperwork."

"A law enforcement official and a cute one to boot…I would not have guessed that."

"I've been on the force twenty-seven years. I became a widower several years back, buried myself in my work after Samantha's death…that has been my normal routine."

"I'm sorry to hear about your wife."

"Don't be. I'm fine. Fond memories of her shall forever remain with me."

"As they should."

Daiquiri's eyes darted toward the door in one last search. A mild disappointment was apparent.

"Sadly, I must tell you again, it is evident that he is not coming."

"Well, it's still his loss…so, twenty-seven years on the force?"

"Yes, twenty-seven long grueling years. Well, it hasn't been all bad. Like any other career, it has its ups and downs. How long have you been practicing law?"

"Heavens no, I'm not a lawyer. I'm a personal assistant to the eldest senior partner at Jacobs & Johnson."

"I see, impressive."

"That's how I'm told to say it in the politically correct arena. Actually, I'm his personal Muse," Daiquiri stated. "I'm telling the truth," she continued in response to Frank's raised eyebrow.

"I've never talked with a real Muse before."

"And, I've never spoken with a real Police Captain before."

"Touché."

"We do what we do."

"How do you assist?"

"Basically," Daiquiri started to explain, "Carver, the partner that hired my services, explains a situation to me and I let him know what I feel about it. From there, he determines which direction to go. People don't know that the Trustworthy Bank deal was purely accepted on the intuition I had."

"Really," Captain North responded, not knowing what to say. "What are your senses telling you about our meeting?"

Daiquiri smiled.

"I sense that you're very much attracted to me," she stated. "You're probably thinking that my statement doesn't support my claim of being a Muse. But, you are attracted to me; your lust for me was, or shall I say is, so great that you broke character and approached me."

Frank still believed that she had not spoken anything earth-shattering.

"And," Daiquiri continued, "you are dying to know if I'd accept your sexual advances."

"Oh?" Frank stated as he rose an eyebrow.

Frank honestly felt that he wasn't being that obvious, but the truth be told, he had already pictured himself smoking a cigarette after their sexual encounter. He had fallen in awe with her.

She's a Zen master, Frank thought because each time she licked her lips, he became aroused, drawn deeper into the desire of her.

"Shall I sex-plore your mind?" Daiquiri asked.

"Sex-plore...it's interesting how you put that."

"This is what your face is showing. It leads me to the possibility of sex-ploring your body."

"What makes you think that I can have sex with a perfect stranger?"

"I could walk out the door and pretend that we've met when I return. Or, you can go with what you feel right now...this very moment."

Oddly, Frank thought about when he had met his wife. How simple those times were and how the dating scene had changed over the years.

Women are aggressive these days, he thought. He looked at her with more than a simple gaze. Frank was captivated by what sat before him. Daiquiri had no trouble recognizing his mild reluctance. Frank hated to admit it, but part of her rebuttal made perfect sense to him, along with the fact that she was even more alluring as she anticipated his response. He made a man's decision. Well, it was similar to the thought that ran through his head, as he attempted to rationalize the notion of sleeping with her.

I am a grown man, damn it, he thought. *I deserve some simple pleasures out of life.*

"What if?" Frank asked. "If I am sexually attracted to you, what would be your answer?"

Daiquiri smiled brightly in an accepting kind of way. "I'd say that this is your lucky day." She let her words linger in the air before continuing with, "Providing your kiss can entice me."

Somehow Frank managed to conceal exactly how much her seductive words made him want to taste her ruby-red lips.

"I have to entice you with a kiss? Here?"

"Now," Daiquiri spoke immediately.

"And if I fail this test?"

"Then you'll never know what our chance meeting might have turned into."

Frank nearly jumped from his seat when her naked foot slowly climbed from the bottom of his pant leg. The motion pushed the material upward until her toes touched his bare skin. The electricity Frank felt was so strong, if a human body had circuit breakers, all of them would have blown. He felt the vibrations from his pounding heart echoing throughout his body. He nodded, accepted the challenge and stood up too quickly. The rapid movement caused the chair leg to sound loudly as it scraped against the tile floor. The awkward sound brought many eyes to their attention. He stood next to her, captivated by her alluring expression, and lowered his head toward hers, uncertain how to proceed. He kissed her red jewels softly, held his lips pressed against hers for a moment. Frank parted his lips, signaling Daiquiri to expect a more passionate one. Instead, Frank seized her bottom lip and held it securely between his teeth. As he gazed into her eyes, he ran his tongue back and forth across the captive lip.

Now, that's different, Daiquiri thought.

Daiquiri enjoyed his playful act, but when Frank took the nail of his pinky finger and ran it down the length of her neck, she knew instantly that he had surpassed the challenge. She felt warm. She was wet, and knew what her answer would be. Frank felt the breeze from her heavy exhale across his lips and understood that something had affected her. He winked before he sat back in his chair.

"How was that?" Frank asked.

Realistically, Frank didn't care what her answer would be. He was riding high, felt a great sense of accomplishment knowing that that was the wildest thing he'd ever done.

"You get an 'A-plus,'" she stated as her arm flew up to grab the waiter's attention. She posed her fingers, scribbled in the air and announced, "Check, please."

Frank was smiling inside, partly because he had made a bold move, but most importantly, he sensed that Jason would be proud of him.

SEVEN

SEVEN

D aiquiri lived in a Southside high-priced townhouse. The area was under renovation. It had been one of the poorest areas in Virginia City, but after tearing down and redesigning the salvageable units, the area was surely blossoming with promise.

Frank was just a few minutes behind Daiquiri. Five minutes to be exact. When he pulled into the driveway, he noticed Daiquiri motioning for him to pull his car into the open side of the double-car garage. She met him at the garage door entrance to the townhouse wearing a blue silk teddy. What struck him as odd was a ninety-nine-cent pair of shower shoes.

"I like to be comfortable," she responded, noticing Frank's attention to them. To her credit, the shower shoes matched the teddy perfectly.

Daiquiri made certain that his vehicle was completely inside the garage, pushed the button to lower the door and then led Frank through the kitchen to the dining room.

"I can see that being a Muse is profitable," Frank said as he scanned her furnishings.

"Jacobs & Johnson aren't my only clients. I have others that use my unique skills...even though Mr. Carver would like to have me at his beck and call."

"It's good to know that you haven't put all of your eggs in one basket."

"A girl can't afford to."

Frank bit the inside of his bottom lip, watched her with uncertainty and pondered the right words to get the evening underway.

"I'm confused," Frank confessed oddly.

"Why do say you that?"

"I know why I'm here, yet I don't know why I'm here." Frank's head shook from side to side. "A riddle within a riddle."

"You're nervous. You're about to say that you don't do these types of things or something of that nature."

"That about sums it up. I always thought that my wife and I would always be together. We used to talk about how we would make love in our eighties. She was my high school sweetheart, my first and my last."

"Is it painful to say her name?"

"No. Her name was Samantha."

"*Is* Samantha," Daiquiri corrected. "She may not be physically here, but she is with you. How else would you explain the thoughts of her when you're about to be with another woman?"

Frank gazed at her with more uncertainty. He was sure he still wanted to be with her, yet a clear answer for her inquiry eluded him.

"Would a drink relax you?" Daiquiri asked.

"Maybe a bit."

"Would you like anything special? Vodka? Gin? I like those straight up and hard...just as I do my men," she joked devilishly.

Frank smiled before he replied, "I'm not that much of a grizzly. I like Vodka with orange juice."

"Ice?"

"Just a little, please."

"In that case, I'll make you a Vodka smoothie."

Frank realized that he had never had a smoothie of any kind. This thought made him wrinkle his forehead.

"Trust me," Daiquiri said, "you'll like it. It is one of my specialties."

She excused herself to the kitchen to prepare the drink. She started with a sixteen-ounce glass filled with ice. She poured the crystal liquid in the glass until the Vodka level was about one-third full and emptied the contents into a blender. She then added an unmeasured amount of orange juice into the blender and a large orange that had been cut into tiny pieces. The top was placed on the glass pitcher. Seconds later the churning and grinding sound of an expensive-looking blender filled the air. When all of the ingredients had been blended into the purest liquid form, she poured a small amount into an eight-ounce glass, tasted the creation, and then blended the beverage for a few more seconds. A moment later, she walked into the family room proudly holding two glasses of what she deemed as a perfect frozen smoothie.

"I know you'll really like this," she said as she passed him a glass.

"Vodka smoothie, huh?"

"You'll like it." As Frank lowered the glass away from his lips Daiquiri asked, "Well?" with a small bit of concern displayed on her face.

"It's good. I'd imagine this is a drink that sneaks up on you?"

"It tends to do that. Would you be surprised if I did the same to you?"

"What exactly would that entail?"

"Darling, it is best if I showed you."

Daiquiri walked Frank into the family room and positioned him in front of a cream-colored leather winged-back chair. She pulled his shirt out of his pants and unbuttoned, removed and tied his shirt around her waist with the shirt's arms. She playfully pushed him down into the seat, walked behind him and began massaging his shoulders. Her fingers were soft, but the pressure she applied to his tight muscles was firm. Frank closed his eyes and tried to remember the sensation of any woman's touch, however, he couldn't consciously recall a moment. Even the feeling of his wife's touch escaped him. The feeling of a female's skin had pretty much faded into a distant memory.

However, as he pleasingly moaned to Daiquiri's gracious massage, he realized that her fingertips felt like electro-pads, each stimulating a nerve. One nerve in particular was the pathway to sensations that he had forgotten he possessed.

"How does that feel?"

Frank tilted his head back the best that he could and replied, "It's difficult to describe the effect your hands have on me."

Daiquiri smiled. She walked in front of him while keeping her soft hands on his shoulders. One of her hands slowly trailed to his chest. Surprisingly, Daiquiri saw that the old man still had remnants of a chest. She could tell he had been fit at one time in his life. His pecs, no longer large, hadn't completely dropped and they still possessed a muscular shape. Most of Frank's chest hairs were gray. She mentally disputed Frank's prior comment about his beer gut, knowing that she'd seen stomachs far worse than his.

"Is this where I lose my virginity?" Frank asked.

"No. This is just an appetizer. A little something to get you thinking about the main course."

"I see."

Without further comment, Daiquiri lowered the zipper and pulled his semi-hard member through the briefs' slit. For the longest time Daiquiri only played with him. She fondled and stroked him for minutes without actually taking her human dildo into her mouth. Frank didn't mind. After his wife died, he performed the self-pleasing act, but as in all things, the thrill went away. Other than holding himself to perform the natural act, his manhood hadn't enjoyed any activity.

He loved the way she teased him and was proud he still had some youth left in him because he felt himself get stronger by the minute. Daiquiri had noticed too. The more she played, the more she felt him become steel-like. She wished she could take all of the credit, but only she was aware that her version of the Vodka smoothie was special.

The Viagra is working, she thought.

She had poured herself the initial glass, crushed one half tablet of Viagra in the remaining drink and blended the drink for a few seconds more. Daiquiri was even more pleased with the confidence that Frank's youthful hard-on gave him. Once she was satisfied that the erection would last, she lowered her mouth onto his anxious tool. Frank's eyes nearly popped from the sockets when she closed her mouth around him. Daiquiri squeezed, teased, licked and sucked her toy until she was very sure that he was about to explode.

She instructed Frank to stand, placed the chair's matching throw pillow on the floor under her knees and proceeded to unfasten his belt. She turned Frank's back to her and lowered to her knees as his pants were pushed to his ankles. She used one hand to stroke his tool like a guitar string while she placed a tiny portion of his briefs between her sharpest I-teeth. With minimal effort, she made a tiny tear in the garment. Tiny for the moment because she put a lone finger into the tear and pulled until there was room for two fingers. She repeated the destruction of the garment until four fingers were through the large hole. The torn material was clenched in a strong fist. Forcefully, she ripped the seat out of his briefs and let it dangle down reminiscent of old-fashioned pajamas that had the rear buttons missing.

Frank didn't know whether or not the sound of her hand spanking his ass was more startling than the act itself. Nevertheless, he looked down with a half-smile filled with excitement.

"Thank you for letting me perform," Daiquiri stated. "It has been quite some time since I've been able to go beyond the missionary position."

Frank believed it was easier to accept that she was a Muse than to believe her last statement. *After all*, he thought. *I'm the one who has mauled briefs.*

Daiquiri hinted that Frank sit. She spread his knees as wide as the cushiony arms of the winged-back chair would allow. She leaned over, placed her head between his legs with each of her hands secured above the left and right knee respectively. She bent both knees, pushed upward with a good amount of effort and sprung into a headstand that an Olympian would admire. She held the position for what Frank counted as three seconds, then fell forward onto his chest. Her inviting haven settled accessible to his mouth. Although he was startled by her acrobatic move, he had to smile when the words "Care for dessert" reached his ears.

Now that's different, Daiquiri thought as she felt a cool breeze on her glistening lips.

Again, she felt the blowing from Frank's mouth, followed by the sound of two different kinds of lips kissing. He parted her with the tip of his tongue, took a slow ride up to her clitoris and circled his wet tongue around it ever so slowly. Frank alternated between darting his instrument of destruction in and out of her haven and wrapping his soothing lips around her object of desire. He continued his manipulations until a delicate passionate cry filled his ears.

"Not like...not like," Daiquiri panted. "Not like this," she continued.

She wanted to be in full ride mode when she came so she somehow lowered herself to the floor while Frank was in the middle of devouring her.

"You do that pretty good," she said while trying to compose herself.

"I just went with the flow," Frank added. "After all, it was you who got me started."

Daiquiri stood in front of Frank with her back toward him. This time she placed a hand on each armrest, lifted herself, and spread her legs across each arm.

"Find the pot of gold," Daiquiri instructed.

With that Frank seized his tool and ran his steel-like manhood through her wetness until he found the wet-box's insertion point. On queue, Daiquiri lowered onto his hardened member.

Daiquiri's antics were a result of her playful mind, but when Frank's tool filled her, the seriousness of their intimate act became apparent. Her eyes opened wide as if she had experienced a strange phenomenon. This phenomenon was exactly what she was feeling. She'd sat backward on a man countless times. It was her favorite position, but with Frank, it was as if he slithered through her body like a snake. She swallowed hard as if preventing herself from choking. However, it didn't stop her from wanting more, even at the risk of damaging her insides.

Frank's confidence was running on an all-time high. Once Daiquiri sat on him, he took over. Daiquiri's joy was ignited by Frank's rock-hard member that suddenly felt indestructible. The more he grinded himself into her jewel, the more it seemed to expand. With the expansion, came a hardness that fueled his confidence more than an aphrodisiac could ever duplicate. Of course, unbeknownst to him, his reaction to the sexual encounter was induced by the Viagra drink. Still, in this case, ignorance was bliss because he was thrilled to be now pounding her from underneath.

With every moan and sound of pleasure that expelled from Daiquiri's mouth, Frank felt in total control. He politely pushed her legs off the armrest and positioned them in front of him on the floor. He placed his palm between her shoulder blades and pushed forward. Daiquiri wouldn't have thought it possible, but leaning forward, Frank got deeper inside her joy. She wanted to cry out, but held the words. She simply took pleasure in what Frank was doing to her.

Frank wanted to release his years of abstinence into her, but all he had was the sensation before the explosion. He tightened his butt muscles with hopes of accelerating his climax; yet the Viagra still had his moment contained. To further enhance the experience, he stood and pounded her from the rear, hard and fast for a long moment. He pushed his knees into the back of hers and slowly lowered them to the floor. He continued his hypnotic movement in full doggie-style position. He stopped the pounding. Sweat poured from his forehead. Sweat ran down his back. Not because he was about to come, but because he was damn tired. Frank did his best to keep the majority of his weight off of her as he rested on all fours with Daiquiri doing the same below him.

Suddenly, Frank's weight on her increased tenfold. Daiquiri had to topple over to the side to prevent being pinned under him.

EIGHT

Frank was out cold. Daiquiri looked up and understood why. Looking down upon her with great disgust was Poncho holding a baseball bat.

"Damn it, Poncho!" Daiquiri screamed. "Couldn't you wait until we finished? I don't like you watching me do the nasty."

"I watch you every time we fuck. So, what's the big deal?" Poncho responded.

"That's different. We only fuck out of habit."

"There ain't no fucking difference other than I don't get sloppy seconds."

Daiquiri and Poncho stood over Frank's unconscious body debating Poncho's timing. Poncho searched Frank's pockets.

"You make me sick," Daiquiri yelled.

This, however, was before Poncho "bitch slapped" her. Daiquiri stumbled, lost her balance and fell across Frank's body.

"I don't know…," Daiquiri stated while picking herself up from the floor. "…what in hell's name has gotten into you?"

Rage radiated from her body like the glow of a full moon, caused by the glowing pain of the birthmark-like handprint displayed so vibrantly on her face. Suddenly the original thought was gone.

"Don't ever put your fucking hands on me again!" Daiquiri screamed. "Or, you'll see how deadly I can be."

"Whatever," Poncho responded nonchalantly.

"You can act like you're not hearing me and not take me seriously, but if you ever," Daiquiri yelled for effect, "hit me again, you'll die where you stand."

"As I said before, whatever bitch!"

Daiquiri shot piercing eyes at him but remained silent.

"Now, what in the hell were you going to say before you lost your mind and started yelling at me?"

"I was about to say that I don't know what you plan to do with him."

"What I always do."

"He is a Police Captain, dumb ass!" Daiquiri felt as though she had slapped him verbally.

A look of amazement decorated Poncho's face. He felt another sudden burst of anger.

"Why in the hell didn't you tell me?" Poncho yelled. "I thought he was Sebastian Cole. I found his card at the other place."

"Think, idiot. We have to be very selective. A Lieutenant Governor is more of a no-no than a Police Captain. I'm not going to jail behind your foolishness. You're going to get us busted. Besides, did I call and tell you that we were on tonight? No!" Daiquiri snapped, without waiting for his reply. "You jumped the gun as you always do."

"But, you let him park his car in the garage," Poncho stated in his defense. He knew that was the usual signal when a prey was in the lair.

"I just wanted to get fucked tonight," Daiquiri confessed. "I just wanted a simple fuck to let my hair down with someone other than you or the real victim who, by the way, didn't show tonight."

"You still should have called me."

She thought, *Asshole*. The thought transferred to her face without speaking the word.

"And," Daiquiri continued, "if we did have a play tonight, I would have called. Have I ever not called you when we had the person we set out to get? You just fucked up. What are you going to do to fix your mess? I just can't tell him, oops, my bad when he wakes."

Poncho looked down at Frank with uncertainty. He knew that cop killing was a serious crime. However, Daiquiri was right. Frank being knocked unconscious couldn't be explained without repercussions.

"I'll do what I need to do and clean this shit up nice and tidy."

When the phone rang, Daiquiri was overzealous with her explanation to the caller that Poncho's boldness had a police captain knocked out on the floor. Poncho knew who the caller was and snatched the phone from her. Poncho explained that his options were very limited and relayed to the caller that they'd wipe the place clean of fingerprints and remove anything that could tie the rented place to them. Although their places of operation were obtained with false identification under the guise of dummy corporations, it didn't sit well with either Poncho or the caller. Poncho tried to appease the caller by stating that they could have a politician in play. The caller agreed with Daiquiri's assessment that ripping off a political figure would surely end their scam. Poncho moved the phone from his ear when the caller yelled and called him a stupid mutha-fucker for knocking a police captain out.

There was a momentary silence that somehow made Poncho nervous. After viewing Frank's police identification, Poncho relayed back per the caller's inquiry that Frank was from the Sixteenth Precinct. Poncho sensed that the caller was in deep thought. Never would he have imagined that he'd hear the words, "Ice his ass." Poncho pulled the receiver from his ear again. This time he gazed at it as if it were a strange object.

"And, don't fuck this up," Poncho heard as the phone was put back to his ear. "He is sure to come out."

Poncho didn't understand nor did he question the last comment.

"Don't worry," Poncho replied. "CSI won't be able to trace the death back to us."

Poncho heard, "Do your thing. Peace out." Then a dial- tone sounded in his ear.

Poncho enlisted Daiquiri's help in putting Frank's clothes back on. Although he would have preferred the non-violent route, the thought of getting back to what he's good at enticed him. He became excited.

NINE

Poncho proved to be strong for his sloppy-looking physique. He muscled Frank's unconscious body into the passenger side of Frank's vehicle and leaned him against the door as if he were asleep. Frank was driven back to Jazzpers parking lot. Although it was near closing time, Poncho parked Frank's car under one of the three lampposts and was lucky enough to get a seat inside with a clear view of Frank. He was confident that he hadn't been seen positioning Frank's body in the driver's seat.

Once inside the club, Poncho pretended to listen to the last set that the live band played, but clearly most of his focus was on looking for signs of Frank's movement.

Come on, Poncho thought impatiently. *Wake your ass up.*

It was as if Frank had been given a direct order. He slowly straightened his hunched-over-the-steering-wheel body to a sitting position. While he couldn't consciously remember how he got to where he was, the surroundings seemed vaguely familiar to him. Frank felt a huge lump at the base of his neck and was sure that it was a blood clot. What he didn't understand was how it got there. He placed both arms around the circumference of the steering wheel, leaned forward and rested his aching head on one of his wrists. After a very short while, Frank thought, *I need medical attention.*

His head felt like it was being blown up from the inside. Yet, it compared little to the explosion that ravaged through Frank's vehicle when he attempted to start it. The car seemed to implode. Flames raced through it rapidly and ferociously. The shattered windows sprayed deadly projectiles in all directions. Frank's body incinerated under the massive heat and flames, almost like an instant cremation.

The explosion rocked the exterior glass of Jazzpers and the remaining patrons watched the barnyard fire from afar. The manager feebly attempted to douse the flames, but the fire would not yield to the white mist of a lone fire extinguisher. He tossed the empty red cylinder to the ground, backed away and waited for the professionals that he heard arriving from a distance. While the firemen put out the flame, a trio of police officers arrived. Two policemen came in a black and white car and Detective Austin from the Sixteenth Precinct was close behind in an unmarked vehicle.

Once the debris had cooled down enough for the Fire Marshall and Forensics team to start their separate investigations, Detective Austin was the first to attempt to dispel his fears. However, Detective Austin already feared the worst. One foot out of his car, a tin sound crackled under his foot. "Frosty," he read. A panic that he's never experienced overcame him so heavily that he had to sit back down inside the car. Detective Austin rubbed his forehead with his fingertips as if they could absorb the thought and the fear. He looked at the license plate once again. Everyone at the Sixteenth Precinct knew that the object blown from Frank's car referred to his gray hair.

"Ten-108! Ten-108!" Detective Austin yelled into the police radio. "Ten-108 at Sixth and Maple streets."

The "Officer Down" distress call multiplied ten fold the amount of police officers on the scene. The initial investigation of the bits and pieces of recoverable evidence from the explosion was gathered and tagged. What little remained of Frank's body was taken to the city morgue. Poncho watched the ordeal with the other nosy spectators.

He chuckled and thought, *You'll never trace anything back to me*.

Poncho was absolutely right. The explosives were made by him thanks to the wonders of the internet. The detonator device used was made of hard plastic and it melted, faded into nothingness well before most of Frank's bones. Nothing was traceable back to him, not even the testimony of an eyewitness who saw the car explode.

Perfect, he thought. He stepped away from the crowd and jumped in the car with Daiquiri with his mind at ease.

TEN

The next day, Michael Jenkins rolled off of Toni Smalls sweating profusely. It wasn't that he'd just spent hours making love to her; actually he'd be lucky if they reached the ten-minute mark. However, his chauvinistic ways made him think that since they both had the same amount of time to reach a climatic state, she squandered her opportunity. He took a deep breath to calm his racing heart.

"That was beautiful...you felt damn good," he stated, still thinking of his explosion.

"Thank you," Toni commented. "I enjoyed myself too," she lied.

"I never dreamed that my day would be like this considering its horrible start. I was happy for your assistance with my broken-down vehicle and all, but having a strange sexual chemistry with you caught me by surprise."

Michael pressed his lips against hers and was about to make the act more passionate when he heard the sound of glass breaking.

"What was that?" he asked already knowing the answer to his query.

"Oh my God! I don't know!" Toni responded in a scared state.

Michael did what any man worth his weight would do. He slipped on his pants and left the bedroom to investigate the disturbance. He looked back and saw Toni entering the bathroom before he stepped out of the bedroom door, then he fell to the floor. He could vaguely hear Toni frantically calling his name when his blurry vision came back into focus.

"Wha...what happened?" he asked as his sense slowly returned to him.

"I don't know who, but someone knocked you out. I saw you step out of the door, then suddenly fall to the floor. You have a nasty bruise on the back of your head and the swelling under your eye seems to confirm my suspicions."

"You weren't harmed?" Michael asked concerned.

"No, I screamed when I saw you fall, ran and locked myself into the bathroom. I yelled to whoever it was that the silent alarm had been tripped and the police were on their way. I heard a ruckus in the bedroom for a couple of minutes...then it was silent for a good while before I came out."

Michael sat up in the spot on the floor. Even though it was only one punch that knocked him out cold, he felt as though he'd participated in a fifteen-round losing battle. His entire body ached.

"Did they take anything?" he managed to ask her.

"My purse is gone and so is your wallet from your pants."

"That's okay, money and credit cards can be replaced. I'm just happy that your quick thinking kept you safe."

He sprang to his feet and somehow managed to make it to the bedroom window. The knockout punch compared little to the "I'm dead" sensation that swept him like massive hurricane winds when he noticed his car missing.

"This can't be happening," Michael stated soberly.

Toni joined him at the window, peeked out and immediately knew his despair.

"Tell me that your car has Lo-Jack or some other anti-theft device," Toni asked him.

"As my luck would have it, I was on my way to have it installed when I got the flat...met you and..."

"I'm so sorry. I'd better call the police."

"No!" Michael said very animated. "I can't have the cops involved, especially here."

Toni's expression dictated that she didn't understand his reluctance to do the right thing.

"You see," Michael continued, "I'm married with two small children, but most importantly, my parole officer can't find out. Outside of the fancy clothes and nice cars, I have a past that I'm desperately trying to separate myself from. Even though I'm the fucking victim, it just wouldn't look good."

"Is there anything that I can do?"

Michael started feeling resentment toward their association, but he held his tongue.

"The best thing you can do is offer me a ride to a neutral place."

"Really, I wish that I could…but my car was stolen too. I can call you a cab."

"You said they took your purse."

"They did, but I have money stashed away. It's the least that I can do."

"Thank you, I'd appreciate it."

Michael took the cab to the nearby Multiplex and used the change to purchase a movie ticket to give him time to compile his thoughts and dream up a believable story for the authorities.

Toni went downstairs, poured herself a glass of wine. She sat at the kitchen table and thought about changing wine brands when the door that led to the double-car garage opened.

"How did it go?" a man about five years her senior asked.

He was Poncho Rizon, Toni's partner in crime. He had fair skin with a nice grade of hair. However, his body showed signs of a man about fifty years old, even though he was years away from that age.

"One punch this time, huh? What have you been doing, pumping iron?" Toni asked.

Poncho supported his potbelly with both hands and lifted it above his belt. "Does this look like I know what a gym is? I do know what a beer is, got any?"

Toni's head jerked twice toward the refrigerator. "You know where it is," she stated.

She left her seat and stood in the doorway of the garage door. The garage housed both her and Michael's cars.

"We should get a pretty penny selling this Jag piece by piece," she heard coming from behind her.

Michael's car was the Jaguar S type 4.0. It was the newer model that for the first time featured standard all-wheel drive. Toni's Mercedes was one that she and Poncho had swindled from another nameless soul. Identical wrecks for each car had been purchased from a junkyard as total losses. The cars were then registered and tagged. The difference was, Poncho's crew knew how to remove the VIN number from the wreck and swap it with the VIN number on the stolen car. Thus, the procedure left them with functional and legal cars to drive.

Toni's perceived wealth, the expensive-looking clothes and the stolen car, was the catalyst that helped Michael trust her enough to follow her home. Her other asset was a five-foot-seven-inch, slender-built frame that brought her plenty of attention from both sexes. As far as she could tell, she was not a descendant of Dorothy Dandridge, but many had sworn that she could pass for a younger sister or daughter. Toni's crime partner, Poncho also possessed a model-looking face although his body told a different story.

Poncho's arms draped around Toni from behind, he cupped both breasts in each hand and kissed her politely on the neck. Toni sighed because his action was a sure sign on what was to come.

"Go clean yourself, you know that I don't like sloppy seconds," Poncho demanded.

"Can I at least take a moment to relax?"

"You know that it bothers me when you're with other men," Poncho stated before he pinched one of her nipples.

Toni excused herself and took the time to pour a tall glass of wine. She drank it straight down as if the elixir would calm her nerves before she headed for the shower. Toni heard Poncho open the bathroom door.

"How much time do you think we have to clean this place up?" Toni yelled from the shower.

"Enough time for you to finish your shower and me to get a quickie. My dick is hard just thinking about it. Actually, the cleanup crew will be here within an hour, so hurry up and bring that sweet pussy to me."

Toni sighed as she turned the water off.

"We have to find a way to swindle people's cars and not have to abandon the place," Toni spoke. "I like this one the best."

"It is nice, but we can't have people coming back with the police after we take their nice cars. It's just an extra precaution."

ELEVEN

"Look at him," Monique told her son Jason. "He is devastated that he can't quickly master this game of golf."

"Do you think it bothers him that much?" her son asked.

"I know so. The one thing that I've learned is Jason is very competitive... especially with himself."

"That part is so true."

Jason Jerrard had his game face on. He went through his mental check-list before slowly taking the golf club back. He was mad at himself and had trouble releasing the thought that he had driven his last tee shot into the trees. As he stood on the next tee-box negative thoughts were present even through his pre-shot routine. *One bad thought begets another bad shot*, Jason's mind tormented him.

Jason came through his tee shot with a heavy pull to the right. He cursed himself again, especially since the errant shot dictated what he deemed as an Easter egg hunt into the trees again looking for his ball. As luck would have it, he found his ball in the deep grass. However, trees obstructed any chance of him reaching the green with the second shot. He assessed the situation and concluded that even with a clear shot to the green, he wouldn't likely make it because of the condition of the thick heavy grass around his ball. He slammed his club into the ground in frustration on the walk back to the golf cart.

Jason switched to the sand wedge, a club that would get the ball up into the air quicker. Back at the ball, he elected to strike his second shot on the par four hole horizontally back to the fairway in order to attack the green with his third shot. He grunted as his club connected and thrashed through the thick grass that grabbed and twisted the club in his hand. As the huge clump of grass fell from his sight, he saw the ball landing safely in the fairway and rest just behind the one hundred-fifty-yard marker.

"Good shot," the junior Jason said to the senior.

As Jason placed the club back into the bag, Monique told him that it was a very smart play.

"Thank you," Jason told Monique. "Placing the ball back in a playable position was pretty much the only option I had."

"Even so, it was well played."

Monique had what Jason described as a slow and steady game. Her struck balls didn't travel a great distance, but you can always count on her being in a position to strike her next shot absent trouble. The younger Jason had youth and flexibility on his side. He was long off the tee and skilled with his irons. However, his major weakness was the short game, the chipping and putting aspects of the game. These flaws usually allowed Jason senior to catch up with him on strokes. Monique and the younger Jason had already played their second shots, each respectively in good position to make par.

Jason senior looked at the pin position on the golf cart. *In the front*, he thought to himself. *I need to be short*, the thought continued. He pulled the eight iron from the bag and took two practice swings while he visualized the stroke he wanted to execute. *Give it more loft*, he told himself. Jason placed the ball in front of his stance instead of the usual two footmarks back from center. He took a deep breath, exhaled slowly to release any possible tension and moved the club at a steady medium away from the ball. When he brought the ball back around at a swift pace, he felt no impact between the club head and the ball. Jason finished his swing, standing tall and well balanced. This was when the arrogant part of his personality took over. Jason turned around without watching the flight of the ball and put the club back into the bag.

"Aren't we full of ourselves today?" Monique asked Jason.

"Why would you say that?" Jason responded as he sat down in the driver's seat of the golf cart.

"You didn't even watch your shot."

"I didn't have to. I could tell it would be good simply by the sound of the impact."

"See, full of yourself."

Jason smiled.

The younger Jason carried his golf bag on his back. He had started walking to the green when he turned and spoke, "You may have saved yourself a dollar with that shot."

"Thank you," the senior Jason responded. "I can't concede to you that easily."

Jason's third shot from the fairway was a great one. The ball landed in the fringe around the green, bounced once and stopped inches from the cup for a "pickup par." Not to be outdone, the junior Jason's third shot rolled within three feet of the cup and he tied Jason with the short par putt. Monique's par putt rolled around the rim of the cup, but failed to fall into the hole. Therefore, she settled for a one over bogey score on the par four hole. Monique hated to admit it, but she enjoyed the minor competition between the two Jasons.

As the older Jason addressed the ball on the next tee, his sensitive ears picked up the vibrating rattle of his cell phone dancing inside a compartment in the golf cart. He waited for the sound to subside, then began the hole. Jason junior had already played.

Jason retrieved his cell phone as Monique took the tee box. He had one missed call, a voicemail message and a text message. He pushed a few buttons and held his breath for a small moment after reading, the *Jason, I'm pregnant* text-message sent by Monique. He watched her hit the golf ball with a huge smile on his face. When Monique sat back in the golf cart, Jason grabbed her soft hand and caressed it tenderly.

"You know," Jason said, "I should be upset with you."

"Why? Is it because I'm just three strokes behind you this round?"

"Now, you're full of yourself. You know very well what I'm talking about."

"Ah? Could you be referring to the fact that we'll be changing diapers soon?"

Jason hugged her tightly for a moment, then diverted to his pet saying, "Excuse me while I dance."

Monique was thrilled that he received the news so well. After all, the news came about six months too early. They both thought it would be best if the birth control pills she had been taking had run their course through her system. Therefore, their method of birth control was foam contraceptive that proved to be no match for Jason's speedy sperm.

Jason jumped from the cart and literally excused himself to dance. Monique laughed as Jason performed his version of the Pee-Wee Herman dance that included mocking the well-known tune.

"It appears that you've told him the news," Monique's son asked standing next to her seated in the golf cart.

"Yes, he knows now."

"Mom, I'm very happy for you two. The special love that you two have makes the gift of a baby even more wonderful. He will make a great father and I have firsthand experience that you're the best mom."

He kissed her politely on the cheek and started the walk to his ball. Monique became filled because of her son's words. Somehow, she was able to hold back the tears.

"Congratulations," Jason told his mentor.

"Thank you, son," Jason responded.

It was the first time that Jason had addressed the boy, now man, who was raised to be in his image as his own. Monique couldn't express how her mate's comment had made her feel or explain the depth of emotions that her son and her man's interaction had given her. All that she truly knew was that she was extremely proud. The uplifting emotion filled her once again, but this time the tears silently rolled down her face. Jason kissed one of the falling tears and whispered to his mate that he loved her.

"Excuse me," Jason said as he attempted to listen to the voicemail.

The voicemail was left by Detective Kevin Austin. The brief message that simply stated "Jason...Kevin...911," told Jason that he wouldn't be able to finish the round.

"What is it?" Monique asked her man after noticing his facial expression.

"I'm not sure," Jason responded. "Whatever it is, it can't be good. Kevin left me a voicemail with an indication that there was some sort of emergency. You and Jason should finish the round, but I have to go."

Monique had seen him tense before, but this time his reaction was different. She knew him well and sensed that he was trying not to show much concern. With her he had failed.

"It's okay," the younger Jason stated. "If we all leave now, I won't run the risk of being late picking up Caramel."

"That's the wise thing to do," Monique agreed. "You should be at the airport early like the gentleman I raised you to be."

"Then it's settled," Jason senior chimed in. "I can make my way to the precinct if my son would be so kind as to drop his mom home."

"Consider it done," the younger Jason stated. "Go handle your business."

"Thank you," Jason replied to the junior. "Those exact words have been told to me by your mother several times."

After Monique was allowed to change into her street shoes, Jason headed for the Sixteenth Precinct. Monique and her son watched Jason drive away.

"Mom, I thought you said he had retired from the force."

"I did and he is." Jason's facial expression turned into one of confusion. It prompted Monique to continue. "I don't know what that's all about. I do know and have been around him long enough to understand when that expression occurs, all parties should step back."

"Do you think it's that serious?"

"I know it is...retirement hasn't taken the detective out of him."

"I'd imagine that will be with him forever."

"Indeed," Monique concurred.

TWELVE

Jason walked into the Sixteenth Precinct for the first time in several months. To him it was like yesterday. All of the familiar sounds and smells reacquainted themselves with him instantly. All of the "Good to see you again" comments from the officers who knew him became more of an annoyance. Jason felt as if he heard "I thought you had retired" once again, he'd punch whomever dead in the mouth.

He found Detective Austin at his desk tapping a pen on a notepad. The notepad contained thoughts of his new case.

"Kevin, old friend," Jason said, "9-1-1 was all I needed to get me here."

"Jas, good buddy," Kevin responded.

Kevin was happy to see him, but saddened by the news that he had to deliver.

"I would have called, but your 9-1-1 distress call demanded my personal attention," Jason said to his friend whose face displayed a serious dose of despair.

"I for one am happy you made the trip," Sgt. Austin responded.

"Although, you know, it takes a lot to get me off the golf course these days."

"Golf?" Kevin sounded surprised. "You hated that game."

"Times change, people change."

Kevin knew by Jason's tone that it was time to get to the origin of his call to him. He took a deep breath, exhaled it heavily as the pen continued to tap on the pad.

"Captain North is dead," Kevin announced somberly.

"What!" Jason bellowed. "You're fucking kidding me."

"Wish that I was. We discovered what little remains of his body last night."

"Little remains," Jason commented with distress. "What does that mean?"

"It means that his car exploded, turned into an incinerator and his body was just about cremated."

Jason looked toward Captain North's office. He could almost hear the Captain telling him to get his ass down there now. But, the reality of the situation was that he would no longer hear those words. He was no longer a police officer and the man he respected so dearly was dead. Jason couldn't explain his own feelings. Somehow, he felt guilty, practically responsible for the Captain's death. Thoughts of, *if I hadn't retired, he'd still be alive*, ran strangely through his mind. He was hurting and a deep guilt consumed him.

Kevin had worked with Jason for years. He sensed by the expression Jason had, exactly what Jason was feeling.

"Don't beat yourself up," Kevin stated as he placed a hand on Jason's shoulder.

It was Kevin's touch that made Jason realize that the precinct was full of vigor with nearly everyone engaged in activities that dealt with the Captain's death. He hadn't seen that much activity since the night he told Captain North that the mayor's wife was in the hospital.

"Tell me, what can I do to help?"

"I don't know...be supportive. At this point we have very little to go on. You see all of the officers working," Kevin stated while his head scanned the room. "For the most part, they are just spinning their wheels. However, even though there are no signs of foul play, it was no accident. The Captain was indeed murdered. The details are sketchy, but a car doesn't burn like that without help."

"Forensics found nothing?" Jason asked surprised.

"Nothing."

"What about devices attached to the engine or starter. Something has to be left behind."

"Believe me; our forensics team is among the best in Virginia. Neither they nor the fire inspector could come up with anything. The fire inspector hinted that the explosive might have been custom made because of the intense heat that it took to make ashes out of most of Frank's body. His belief was more than one explosive under the car's hood and that Frank had to be covered with a volatile flammable substance of some kind."

"What happened to the good old days when we could easily identify C4, detonator devices and such?"

Kevin's shoulders shrugged as in *don't know*.

"Frank was identified how?" Jason asked.

"Dental records and get this, by the serial number from the engine block. The VIN number on the dash had burned to nothing."

"Who would harm such a gentle man?" Jason asked somberly, without needing a response.

"Your guess is as good as mine."

"How are you holding up?"

"I'm troubled just like you, but I'm managing. Everyone is shaken up."

"He was a great man," Jason stated proudly. "Most of all, he was my mentor. I'll never forget that. Don't get too upset and fall off of the wagon," Jason suggested. "You're looking great. The diet agrees with you."

Kevin felt a sense of pride, a pride that had been absent since Jason's retirement. He recalled that Jason's words had provided him the strength to diet, and he felt more elated that Jason had noticed the weight loss.

"Naw," Kevin boasted. "I'm on it for the long haul. I even have a small exercise regimen."

"Good. I'm proud. Remember, if there is anything that I can do, I'm at your disposal."

"Thank you, but enjoy your retirement. There aren't many people that can kick back in their forties."

"I was probably born to be a detective and will always be. It's just in my blood." Jason cupped his hand over his mouth, ran it down across his chin three times in secession. "First Alfredo, now Frank. Seems like all people I care about are harmed?"

"Jas, it's just a coincidence."

Jason elected not to tell Kevin of the note in his mailbox. He didn't want anyone snooping around in his business while he snooped around Captain North's death.

"Hey," Kevin stated in an attempt to brighten the somber mood. "Do you like your desk?" he asked while nodding in the direction where Jason used to sit.

Jason smiled half-heartedly when he noticed that the desk had the American flag painted over the entire desktop. Centered in the middle of the flag was a smaller painted Superman emblem. A thin sheet of glass protected the artwork.

"Some things never die," Jason commented.

"You don't get it, do you?" Kevin asked. "All joking aside, you made quite an impression here. Believe me, most of the officers would never admit it, but we all strived to be like you...as you were as a detective."

Jason's facial expression turned into one of surprise.

You've come a long way, baby, he thought.

"Listen," Kevin continued, "we decorated your desk, and treat the privilege of someone sitting there as an honor. There is a vote amongst the guys to determine if someone has gone beyond the call of duty. Whoever gets the most votes is allowed to sit there for one month. It has become a status thing to sit at that desk now."

"I'm shocked and amazed," Jason commented. "Most people thought I was an arrogant SOB...well, that's the impression I got."

"Closet admirers, I'd imagine. And, you can be that arrogant SOB when it suits you."

Jason only smiled.

THIRTEEN

Jason junior arrived at the airport one-half hour early. He eagerly waited for Caramel's plane to arrive. He took the moment to reflect on the two and one-half days they had spent together. Their conversation on the ferry had exposed the many things they had in common. They both loved the outdoors and nature. Because of this, Jason had a slew of outside activities planned that he was sure she'd enjoy. He couldn't help but think about the hours prior to his leaving Puerto Rico. How wonderful the intimacy between them had been. He felt they were a perfect union of man and woman mentally and intimately. He had a great sense that her visit would continue to justify the warmth between them spiritually.

About ten minutes left, he thought upon reading that her plane had landed.

When Caramel exited the jetway, his heart raced with the anticipation of another embrace. She too felt a certain exhilaration as she quickened her pace for his touch. She stopped inches in front of him, dropped all bags and draped him in a lustful hug. Their lips locked. The kiss immediately became a deep passionate one that drew attention from all around. Jason broke the kiss energized by the moment.

"I miss you too," Jason stated. He felt a little flushed. "It has been a long three weeks and the time couldn't have passed quick enough for me."

"I know, talking to you on the phone gave me greater anxiety while I waited to come here. So, what's the game plan?"

"First, welcome to the Washington, D.C. Metro area. Virginia City, where we are staying, is on the outskirts of D.C. There is plenty to do here, but let's get you settled. Then we'll see if jetlag has you too tired for activities today. How was the flight?"

"It was long, but uneventful."

Jason picked up Caramel's bags. She hooked her elbow with his as they headed for the car. Jason placed the two pieces of luggage in the backseat of his car.

"I have to move my junk from the passenger seat," Jason said.

He opened the door for her, picked up a long rectangular box and held her hand as she sat. Before closing the door he gave Caramel the box of red and white long-stemmed roses.

"These are for my delicious Caramel," Jason Jr. commented.

"Come here you," Caramel demanded after realizing what the box contained.

Jason followed her inviting index finger all the way to her lips. In a short instant, the simple thank-you peck became one filled with passion, filled with lust of a time gone by, yet an ever present remembrance.

"You'll get yourself in trouble like that," Jason spoke after the kiss ended.

"As I remember it, our first kiss is what propelled us to our first intimacy together."

"True. What a time that was."

They simultaneously blushed upon reflecting on the passion they had shared.

"So, what have you been doing with yourself?" Caramel asked.

"Just spending some time with my mom and my…" Jason paused.

Caramel's head turned toward the younger Jason, intrigued by the sudden pause in his words. "What's wrong?" she asked.

"Nothing. I just realized that it's the first time that I've thought of my mom's Jason as my dad."

"What is so strange about that?"

"I briefly touched on it while in Puerto Rico. I was raised to be like him or my mom's perception of him."

"Do you think she succeeded?"

"It's hard to tell. He is well spoken, dresses nicely, and yet he acts like a clown most times. I guess those things are a part of me, but I draw the line with the no-jeans attitude. I'm most comfortable in those."

"Maybe your mom just wanted you to know that about him," Caramel responded.

When they arrived at Jason and Monique's home, Jason took Caramel's bags to the guest bedroom where she immediately began to unpack. He watched her perform her chore as if the week-long vacation would become an extended one.

"I see you're like most women," Jason spoke.

"I know that I've packed too much, but it is better to have than to have not."

"You did forget something," Jason commented in a serious tone.

Caramel looked at the toiletries that she unpacked, glanced at her items hanging in the closet and ruffled through the undergarments that were tossed on the bed.

"No," Caramel replied. "I have everything. Even tampons just in case Aunt Flow wants to visit early."

"Where's the kitchen sink?" Jason joked. "That's a lot of stuff."

"Boy, I don't know why I took you seriously. Is the older Jason's sense of humor odd like yours?"

"Oh, I hope not."

Jason seized her soft hand, pulled her near and gave a tender hug that was long and endearing. He looked squarely into her eyes.

"I'm so happy you're here," Jason conveyed with emotion.

"I've missed you too," Caramel replied.

The kiss that followed was filled with passion. Partly because they did miss each other, partly because they'd spent countless hours on the phone talking, but mainly because at that very moment they felt connected. The kiss contained that very sentiment.

Jason's heart raced when he heard a slight tap at the open door. Their heads turned quickly to greet Monique standing at the entrance boasting a huge smile. Monique winked at her son before asking Caramel how her flight was. Caramel's embarrassed reply was exactly what Monique sought. She wanted to know if Caramel had any shame in her game. Monique sensed that she did.

"There is a light snack waiting for you two in the kitchen," Monique said. "Come down when you're settled."

"Yes, Ma'am," both Jason and Caramel replied together.

"Ouch," Jason expressed, startled by Caramel's punch in his stomach.

"You're going to get me in trouble and have her hate me before I get a chance to know her."

"Don't worry about that. My mom's cool."

"You'd better be right or I'm going to punch you again."

Jason's second kiss was a polite peck on Caramel's cheek before he assured her that everything was going to be okay.

FOURTEEN

Jason left the station disturbed by the news of Captain North's death. He didn't know where to start. He was uncertain of how helpful he could be, but he knew that he would do something. Jason, as in most times when troubled, found peace, a sense of comfort at Rosalina's. Everyone knew that it was his favorite spot, but even more so now because he was an equal owner along with Alfredo.

Jason and Alfredo made no major changes as the new owners. They kept the restaurant's atmosphere the same instead of altering the special ambiance that the restaurant had always possessed. They did, however, add a canopy that stretched down the steps and ran along the front of the building to keep the line that was forever present shielded from the elements.

Ownership has its perks. Jason reserved his favorite booth for him, and or his guests permanently. Delia had replaced Alfredo at the podium. Retired from her previous life, she was happy to be in the company of her soon-to-be husband, Alfredo. Alfredo had told her that she didn't have to work, but she wanted to contribute.

Jason's newest thing was flavored coffee; therefore, the other perk that he loved best was a tall metal coffee pot which sat on the table. It had a rectangular magnet attached to it for him to write which flavor he'd like to drink. Jason turned the cylinder around to face Delia after writing his choice with an erasable marker.

"I've noticed that you change flavors every time," Delia remarked upon viewing the words "French Vanilla."

"Variety is the spice of life."

"You got that right, but I'll stick with my man. He does right by me."

If Delia hadn't smiled, he would have let the comment go without further thought. But, her devilish grin propelled the word "nasty" into his mind.

"Well," she said, prompted by Jason's expression, "I have a good teacher."

"Both of you should be ashamed of yourselves," Jason joked as Delia turned to walk away.

Jason sat in his booth alone, but not lonely. The fresh love displayed between Alfredo and Delia brought on thoughts of his precious Monique. He missed her; yet these precise thoughts comforted him and gave him a quiet peace inside. He needed that right now because looming in his subconscious mind were thoughts of Frank's death. He closed his eyes, inhaled slowly as if he were consuming her essence. Then he opened his eyes, exhaled even slower and felt that he'd accomplished feeling her very presence.

As Jason bathed in thoughts of Monique, ever so slowly as the hours passed, thoughts of Frank's death crept back. Jason released the thoughts to his conscious mind; at the same time he released the denial of what he needed to do. He reflected on his and Captain North's many years on the force and had finished his food without realizing that he had eaten. The thought that plagued him was his likely return to the police force. Jason believed deeply that the death of his mentor, his friend, required his personal attention. The unanswered question was how would Monique handle the news?

Jason had a brief conversation with Alfredo before leaving the restaurant. One that revealed Delia and Alfredo's wedding arrangements had progressed further than his and Monique's plans. At first he was surprised, but in hindsight, he wasn't. Alfredo and Delia were like two lovebirds, inseparable since their first intimate act. He pushed Rosalina's double doors to exit as if opening them would be the gateway to the truth behind Frank's murder.

Jason knew when he returned home that he'd have a difficult time disguising his turmoil to the woman who knew him best. He walked into his home and found Monique, Caramel and the younger Jason sitting at the kitchen table. Even though he gave Caramel a welcome hug and Monique a peck on the lips, Monique understood that her man was troubled. Jason held Monique from behind, rubbed her stomach with his right hand and whispered softly into her ear.

"I hope I don't drive you crazy doing this until the birth of our child."

"That wouldn't bother me at all," Monique responded. "Let's go upstairs for a minute," she suggested.

Before Jason had time to protest, Monique grabbed his hand and started the trip upstairs. The younger Jason remained at the table with Caramel. He explained to Caramel that they were expecting.

"Isn't your mom a bit old to be having a child?" Caramel asked.

"That's what love does. You've seen them; they're like two pigs in slop when together."

"They are surely a happy couple," Caramel responded even though thoughts of Monique's age plagued her.

Monique entered the bedroom with a most curious expression.

"I need to ask you something," Monique said.

Jason wrinkled his forehead, concerned by the slight anxiety of her voice, but he waited for her to continue.

"Are we having a bastard-child?" Monique questioned with a serious tone and unexpectedly.

"Bastard-child?" Jason responded a bit dumbfounded. "Why would you ask that?"

Monique gazed at him and remained silent.

"No, sweetheart," Jason continued after further consideration. "Our child will not be born out of wedlock. I promise you this."

"You know I'm not pressuring you to marry me because my heart goes well beyond that. But, if we are getting married prior to childbirth, I just need to know if I'll need one of those newer pregnancy-friendly wedding gowns."

"You won't need that. Speaking of which, the two people I know who are nastier than you have already started planning their wedding."

"Who might that be?"

"Alfredo and Delia. Alfredo told me they are planning a fall wedding."

"Good for them. And," Monique said with a huge grin, "I left a web address on the keyboard in your office. I'd like you to view the gowns I've been looking at. Read my scribbled notes and you'll understand why I asked about the pregnancy-friendly dress."

"Do you want me to go look now or after the talk that you really want to have?"

"Go now. You look as though you need to give your mind a little mental relaxation. Afterward, we'll talk about Kevin's call if you're up to it."

Jason sat at his computer and slid the note from the keyboard to the desk. As he typed the web address www.therezfleetwood.com into the browser bar, he pronounced each letter aloud as he pressed the keys. *Therez Fleetwood*, he thought. *That name has uniqueness about it.*

When the web page displayed, it became very apparent that Monique had done extensive research to find a wedding gown designer that suited her distinctive taste. The most surprising thing was Jason actually spent time viewing all of the original wedding gown creations in the four galleries on Therez's website. He was impressed with the variety of styles. Each style was unique in its own way and had intricate details that made each gown a singular entity. Each gown spoke to him, different yet all appealing. He was partial to a gown that was cut above the knee. As soon as he saw it, he pictured Monique's legs accented by the delightful piece. Jason made a mental note of the gown's number, then closed the web page with the understanding that whatever Monique chose to wear for their wedding, he would not be disappointed.

Jason rejoined Monique in the bedroom. She was sitting on the bed flipping through a magazine.

"Did you see anything that you liked?" Monique asked without taking her eyes from the magazine.

"You're very funny. You know very well that many of Theresa's..."

"Therez," Monique corrected.

"Anywho, there are many designs that speak your name."

"I hear several calling me now. Listen," Monique joked. She cupped a hand at an ear. "Monique...Monique..."

She laughed at her own candor.

"We will definitely contract her to design your wedding dress," Jason stated. "And after seeing those gowns, I can't picture you in one of those pregnancy wedding gowns."

"I don't know," Monique joked. "I don't plan to eat for two. I'll be all stomach; therefore, I may not look too bad."

Jason smiled because of the visual picture Monique gave him.

"Now, are you okay?" Monique asked. She changed the subject and her tone.

"Yes, why?"

"Now, you're the funny one. How did it go at the station?" Monique asked Jason. She knew that he was in-tune with her thoughts. "Why the distressed call from Kevin?"

Jason's gaze back was more through her than at her. He felt like he had been hit in the chest. He inhaled deeply and realized that his discomfort was caused by the stress from Frank's death. There was no easy way to relay the information to Monique. Talking about death never was easy for him, especially when it related to a close personal friend. Therefore, Jason spoke the tragic news as therapy for himself.

"Captain North has been murdered," Jason somberly said with saddened eyes.

Monique's eyes closed. She held them shut briefly as if when they opened, Jason's words would be different. When her eyes met his, she understood everything Jason's eyes told her.

"I'm so sorry," Monique said before wrapping her arms around him. "Are you okay?"

"I will be. I'm just shaken by the unexpected news."

"I'm sure Kevin has an investigation going, right?"

"Yes, Frank's murder investigation is well on the way."

"Is there anything that I can do to make you feel better?"

Once again Jason looked through her as he pondered his reply.

"Understand," Jason stated in response to her question.

Monique stood in front of him rubbing a comforting hand through his hair. Jason's simple word commanded her to sit next to him on the bed.

She rested her head against his shoulder in silence. As if the move had been rehearsed a thousand times, Jason instinctively began tenderly stroking her face.

"When are you going to start?" Monique asked the question that disturbed her most.

If Jason had any doubts about Monique's knowledge of him, all uncertainty had been erased. She knew that Jason wouldn't sit idly and let Frank's death go without his involvement. She understood that his mind was set. The tell-all sign was the sad, yet determined puppy dog-eyed expression Jason had when he spoke the word "understand." There was no question that they knew each other well. There was no doubt that she would fight for what she wanted.

"Can't you just let the others handle the investigation?" Monique asked. "The people investigating the murder are all capable. Why don't we just enjoy ourselves without those types of worries?"

"We've had a wonderful early retirement. Everything has been perfect up until a few days ago. The note, Frank's death, what's next? I'll need my senses sharp to handle whatever is forthcoming behind the note. Investigating Frank's death is a means to stay sharp and on my toes."

"Jason, my love, I'm very much aware of what Frank meant to you. I'm hoping that other things are more important to you now that you're off the force...me...our baby. We're going to need you around and at my age, I don't need the stress of wondering about your safety."

"I deeply know that you're concerned about potential harm coming my way, but just know that I'll be okay. Our baby and most importantly, you will have me. Frank was a dear friend as well as a father figure in more ways than I can count. He needs me."

"He is already dead!" Monique spoke with tenacity.

A bass drum echoed through Jason's body. The vibration was a result of Monique's first angry words ever spoken to him. Disappointment in his predetermined decision was behind her unexpected aggression.

Jason wished for a balance, a medium ground that would please both him and his fiancée. Monique's release gratified her; yet she feared the comment may have hurt Jason's feelings. She feared that Jason's return to the force might be a dangerous one, and his need to solve his friend's case could hinder her, his and their child's future.

Money doesn't buy happiness, she thought upon realizing that Jason wouldn't be fulfilled until he solved Frank's murder.

"How about just being a consultant on the case?" Monique stated as a compromise. "This way, you will not have to officially rejoin the force. Your retirement ceremony will not have been wasted."

Jason listened to Monique's compassion that carried a bit of regret even in her compromise attempt. He kissed her on the cheek.

"I'll check into that," Jason responded. "After all, I am Virginia City's Boy Wonder. If I'm allowed to participate in the investigation without reinstating my detective status, I'll do that."

"Thank you. I just have a funny feeling about this," Monique commented.

"I love you," Jason responded. He commanded her attention with his eyes. "Know that, you, our baby and I will be safe," Jason confidently stated.

That was the thing that Monique liked about Jason's character. Years ago and still today, he had the ability to be confident, cool and cocky. Conviction in what he spoke was ever present.

FIFTEEN

Monique and Jason were the ideal couple. Even when things bothered them, they refused to let others know there was strife between them. Therefore, when they rejoined the younger Jason and Caramel in the kitchen, no signs of the tension between them existed.

"What are you guys getting into?" Jason asked the junior.

"We were just discussing that. A bike ride sounds good, that is if Caramel isn't too tired from the flight," the younger Jason responded.

"Bike ride?" Monique questioned her son. "Let the poor girl get some rest. Long plane rides can be exhausting."

"Ms. Monique," Caramel responded. "I'm not that far gone. Something invigorating like a bike ride will surely help me sleep later."

"May we use your mountain bikes?" Jason junior asked.

"Feel free to use anything here," Jason responded. "Our home is your home."

Monique blushed internally. She turned her head away from them to hide the warm flushed feeling Jason's comment gave her.

"Oh," Jason continued. "The bike rack for the car is in the right corner of the garage."

"We will be back later. We're headed for the movies," Monique said.

"To see what?" Caramel asked.

"This time, we're going to live on the edge a bit and choose the movie when we get to the theater," Monique joked.

The movie was to be relaxation for Jason and Monique; a mental getaway to take their minds off of the lingering troubles, at least for a couple of hours. Therefore it mattered little which movie they viewed. The only requirement was a large screen, stadium seating and Dolby surround sound. The AMC Hoffman 22 theater was a short drive from Jason's home.

As for the young couple, they went upstairs to change clothes for the bike ride. A few moments later, at the garage entrance, Caramel was in awe with what she saw. Sitting in the garage was a new Corvette coupe, a convertible Chrysler Crossfire SRT, and a new Pontiac Solstice, the vehicle they would be using.

Jason Jr. knocked over a brown office box while retrieving the bike rack and asked Caramel to replace the items that fell from it. She placed the contents back in the box, one by one. She suspiciously looked over her shoulder for a brief moment to check on Jason upon reading an item that caught her eye. It was a VCR tape with the markings of "Sex tape." The mental note she made was strong, one that would draw her thoughts back to it.

Caramel's Jason drove her to the overlook at Reagan National Airport just outside of Washington, D.C. They were two of many who brought bikes to either take the ride to Old Towne Alexandria or take the bike trail into Washington.

"Let's go that way," Caramel suggested as she pointed her arm in a direction without rhyme or reason.

"Old Towne it is," Jason commented.

The bike path to Old Towne was long, windy and hilly. By the time they reached the waterfront, Caramel's legs were well beyond aching. They rested at the water's edge near the Charter House Seafood Restaurant, the place where they would dine. Jason's attention focused on the odd-looking tree that seemed to have grown out of the water. The tree was on the water's edge. It had an unusually large-sized tree trunk, however, several humongous tree roots spawned from it like octopus tentacles that fed a good distance over, then down into the water. Seemingly, drawing a life-line from the water it fed on. Jason invited Caramel to join him as he stood on a strong-looking tree root. He performed a delicate balancing act as he walked on the tree root, balanced by a tree branch that hung overhead.

"I'll pass," Caramel stated. "I'll get wet for true."

"I understand. The water here compares little to the emerald blue water that surrounds Puerto Rico."

"This is cool though. This area has class. Besides, being here with you makes everything better."

"That's sweet," Jason replied as he made his way back to dry solid ground. He gave her a peck on the lips, and looked into her eyes to let her know how much he adored her. What he saw was a troubled and confused expression fighting to damper her beauty.

"What's wrong?" Jason asked.

"I'm just wondering what does your dad do for a living?"

"He was a detective. Now he and my mom are retired. Why?"

"Three nice cars, plasma TV's and touring the world for well over a month, something is going on with them."

"All I know is they came into some serious money a while ago."

"I see," Caramel pondered. "Is there something that I should know about you?" she asked in another tone and another demeanor.

Her mannerisms became something of a defensive posture. Jason had no explanation for her mood swing. He was lost for a response.

"I...I," Jason stuttered. "What more could I possibly tell you? Every day, every hour and every minute of our time together in Puerto Rico I was completely honest with you about everything."

"May I ask you a serious question?"

Jason began to feel uneasy about the turn the conversation had made. Especially knowing that he had been the perfect gentleman. *Listen to what people have to say*. His mom's words flashed through his mind like the rapid flicker of a strobe light. The thought helped him hold his words with an uneasy anticipation. He nodded in concurrence.

"Are you a sex-maniac or sex-aholic?"

It wasn't his mom's words or words of wisdom from anyone else that contained his laughter...well, he didn't know why the violent roar stirring inside of him hadn't escaped. It just didn't. Jason managed to smile.

"I wouldn't consider myself either one of those. At the age of twenty-seven, my sex drive is strong but not..." Jason paused as he searched for the proper word. "Problematic," he continued.

"But, you've made a sex tape?" Caramel asked with certainty.

The gum flew out of Jason's mouth like a deadly projectile. It splashed into the water, created a small crater before the water filled it, loosing the gum forever. Like the gum, Jason wished that he could have lost the laughter that was exuberating from him. But, it carried on until he truly realized that Caramel was serious.

"What are you talking about?" Jason asked as his joy began to end.

"I saw a VCR tape marked, 'Sex tape.'"

"I know of no such tape. I'm not into that kind of thing. I only have clothes in the bedroom that I'm staying in. It could only be Jason's and my..."

Jason sliced his words as if saying the word Mom would make the accusation true.

"Where did you see this tape?" Jason asked.

"In the garage when I was putting the things back in the box that you knocked over."

"You're positive that it read 'sex tape'?"

"I struggle with speaking English at times, but I read it very well."

"I know that it's not mine, and my mom filming herself doing the nasty... well that's downright disgusting. Yuck!"

Caramel chuckled over the use of Jason's childlike word. Her glee at his expense became contagious. Jason joined in with laughing at himself.

SIXTEEN

Jason and Monique left the theater pleased with seeing the movie *Crash*. They both agreed that the movie depicted real-life situations, but in a dramatic fashion. They were hugged up like two teenagers with a puppy-love crush, engaged in a conversation about the movie when they came across a man sitting on the curb next to the wheelchair ramp. They crossed the street to the parking lot and then Jason whispered something into Monique's ear. Jason walked back toward the man; he took money from his wallet and hid it in the palm of his hand. The man was dressed rather nicely, but his head hung low because of self-pity.

"Tough day?" Jason asked as he sat next to him on the curb.

What now? the man thought. His position remained unchanged except for the slow nod he gave for a response.

"Listen, I don't plan to be a pain," Jason continued. "There was something about your body posture that made me think that you could use a word of encouragement."

"Oh?" the man replied. "What makes you my Guardian Angel?"

Michael Jenkins turned his head toward Jason for the first time. Neither the shame of what had happened to him earlier nor the shame of his black eye prevented Michael from perceiving Jason as his newest nuisance. Under the nighttime conditions and up close Jason could see Michael's eye brilliantly. Rembrandt had painted via Poncho's fist a perfect half-moon that was deep purple in color. It surely looked black to Jason, yet he was able to hold the questions that he had about it.

"I'm not trying to be your Guardian Angel or your Savior," Jason spoke. "I simply thought that if something good happened to you, that maybe it could add a bright spot, however small, to your day."

Michael wasn't in the mood to hear more. His day had been filled with unexpected twists. He thought, *why should I treat your intrusion any differently?* Michael let out a curious sigh.

"What wonderful words of encouragement do you have for me?" Michael asked with a bit of sarcasm.

"Use these to clean your pants," Jason stated while he handed Michael two vertically folded one hundred-dollar bills.

Michael lowered his head again. His eyes were affixed on the pavement. "Thanks," Michael said.

Michael paid no attention to the amount of the money given to him. He unfolded the bills and replaced the vertical fold with a horizontal one.

"I can't replace my car with this," Michael spoke his subconscious thought unknowingly.

"What was that?" Jason asked.

"I said, thank you for your generosity."

When Jason made mention of a replacement car, Michael's demeanor changed slightly. It indicated to Jason that the black eye and a possibly stolen car were related.

"I can help," Jason said. "I'm a cop."

Monique came and stood next to the men just as Jason offered Michael a chance to talk about the incident at the Ruby Tuesday's restaurant behind them. Michael then glanced at the amount of money given to him.

"Okay," Michael agreed.

Michael thought about Jason being a police officer and hoped that he would be able to convince his parole officer that he was the victim. Monique sat at the table and listened to the exchange between the two men. She wasn't a detective, but she believed that Michael's explanation about what had happened to him was so farfetched, that it had to be true.

Jason flipped over a placemat. He wrote detailed notes of Michael's account of his robbery. Michael retrieved an ice cube from his glass and began rubbing it on a burn on his right hand. He made tiny circles around a decorative marking. Jason had all of the information that he needed including Michael's parole officer's contact information. The men stood and shook hands. It was then that Jason noticed the marking that commanded Michael's attention.

"Where did you get that?" Jason asked.

"Whoever knocked my ass out decided that that wasn't enough. The fucker branded me with something." Jason turned Michael's wrist upward and immediately knew what he had seen. The marking branded on Michael was still swollen, apparently still filled with pus, but the circular branding contained legible letters of "VCPA" enclosed in the circle.

"I don't know what this signifies," Michael stated.

Jason reached into his wallet, pulled out a card that he had cherished for years. Jason showed Michael his "honor card" that indicated he was top in his graduating class from the Police Academy. The embossed background was identical to Michael's hand.

"Your case just took on a whole new meaning," Jason stated concerned. "A person only gets this by graduating from the Virginia City Police Academy."

"I was attacked and robbed by a policeman," Michael asked more animated.

"Active, retired or just a fluke...I don't know but, I aim to find out."

Michael was happy with Jason's enthusiasm, yet one question bothered him. "You'll handle my parole officer?" Michael asked.

"Consider it done," Jason assured.

Jason surprised Monique by calling Detective McAllister to the restaurant to take the lead in the investigation. He gave Detective McAllister his notes. Jason and Monique left them at the table with Michael once again rehashing his incident.

On the drive home, Monique was happy that Jason turned the control of the investigation over to Chris, yet she was very curious as to why.

"The last person I'd ever think you'd call would be Chris," Monique stated.

"This is his forte," Jason responded short of laughing. "He is very capable of handling this. It seems very straightforward. However, investigating the possibility of officers committing robberies, that could be a lot of fun."

"Ah, so Frank's murder no longer holds your attention?"

Jason was almost appalled. He knew that Monique understood him better than that. He hadn't mentioned the murder case further because of Monique's reservations about him being involved with it.

"You have to know that my not talking about it is for your benefit," Jason stated.

Monique's eyes locked with his. She appreciated his honesty, but was displeased with what Jason followed with.

"I've heard back from the commissioner," Jason stated evenly. "I can't be involved with Captain North's murder unless I'm reinstated back on the force. Otherwise, according to them, I'd be just a vigilante seeking justice."

Monique's eyes dove deeper into his. Yes, there was no question that she knew her man. She understood—even though it put a sour taste in her mouth—Jason had already decided to officially rejoin the force without input from her. Nevertheless, she decided from their last conversation about the subject matter that she had their baby to think about. Therefore, she would control the things that she could control and not get bogged down with the added emotional distress. Jason's decision to rejoin the force was something that she had no control over, yet she could control how she responded to his decision. Her words were supportive, even though they weren't exactly heartfelt.

"When do you start?" Monique asked.

"I'm signing the necessary papers in the morning," Jason replied.

"I'm confident that someway, somehow, you'll find whomever was behind Frank's murder."

"You can count on that."

Jason held her in a tender comforting embrace. "Please forgive me for not telling you about my reinstatement plans earlier...understand that it is something that I must do."

"I understand, so again, handle your business. Our baby loves you through my love for you. And, honestly, I'm happiest when you're happy."

"Is this why I love you so?"

"Nope," Monique spoke quickly. "You love me because I'm the only one on God's Earth that puts up with your shit."

"Shame on you for putting me out there like that," Jason joked. "Am I a heavy burden?"

"Yes," Monique responded seriously. "But, I have strong shoulders."

SEVENTEEN

The next morning Monique's son was sitting at the kitchen table sipping on a freshly brewed cup of coffee. He'd had a restless night because of his thoughts. He had questions and needed answers about the tape; even though a good part of him felt that it was none of his business. But, it was his mom, the person he had idolized for years.

When he saw Monique walk into the kitchen, her words of always having an open relationship with her rang vividly throughout his mind.

"Good morning, Mom."

"Good early morning," Monique responded. "It is just after five a.m. I don't remember you ever being an early riser."

"Normally, I'm not. You should remember how hard it was to get me up for school. I couldn't sleep." He lowered his head.

Monique let her son's words hang in the balance for a small moment. She studied his face and noted the tone of his voice. She poured herself a cup of coffee and sat across from him at the kitchen table.

"One of those talks, huh?" Monique asked.

"Yeah," Jason responded without realizing that he hadn't used the proper form of the word "yes" with the reply to his mother.

"Caramel's visit not going as expected?" Monique asked.

"Mom," Jason Jr. poised. "I'm more concerned about you, better yet; I have issues about what you're doing."

"Me!" Monique responded surprised. "What on Earth has your underwear in a knot?"

Jason viewed his mom uncertain of how to proceed.

"Are you…," Jason Junior spoke slowly, "making sex tapes with Jason?" her son continued in a rushed manner.

"What!" Monique replied even more astounded.

Monique found herself being the only one amused and tailed off her chuckle with the seriousness of her son's continued gaze into her eyes.

"You're serious, aren't you? What makes you ask such a strange question?"

Monique's child took the VCR tape from his lap and placed it on the kitchen table between them. He found the tape in the exact location where Caramel told him.

"This represents a sex tape that I'm in?" Monique asked her son.

"You tell me, I'm too embarrassed to watch it."

"Where did you get this?"

"It was in a box that I accidentally knocked over while getting the bike racks."

"My dearest son," Monique stated with a serious tone. "I don't know anything about this tape. I do however know someone who does."

"Jason," both Monique and her son responded together.

Monique slowly pulled the tape to her with one hand and placed the other hand onto her son's hand.

"Don't worry," Monique comforted her child. "Rest your mind. I'm not as freaky as you've made me out to be," Monique joked.

The younger Jason faked his best laugh. He recognized his mom's attempt to lighten the mood, but twenty-seven years with her had given him the wisdom to know when she was troubled. He stood, gave her a caring hug and headed back to his room without saying anything further.

Monique found the strength to finish her coffee before going to the basement to view the tape.

Technology is confusing, Monique thought while viewing all before her. There was a sixty-three-inch, high-definition plasma television, HDTV DVD player, expensive Bose surround sound system with a separate tuner, but no VCR to be found. She recalled hearing Jason say something about recording the few shows that he watched on the high-definition DVR. The programs on this device were saved directly to hard drive, virtually eliminating the need for a VCR. She sat on the loveseat and tapped the VCR tape continuously in the palm of her hand.

"Ah," she said aloud, then made her way upstairs.

Located in the smallest of the four bedrooms was a TV/VCR combination unit. When she turned on the TV the volume was startlingly loud. Monique quickly silenced the noise and listened carefully for sounds of someone, particularly Jason. Monique closed the door but didn't shut it all of the way.

The tape started with a camera's view of a bed inside the cabin of a vehicle. Next you saw the door opening with Jason standing alongside a woman. The next scene was one that Monique disliked. Her man was tied to the bed with a woman clawing all over him. Monique's mood became extremely tainted when Jason and the woman kissed, but seeing the woman lower herself onto Jason's manhood, it all but crushed her.

As the squeal of the bedroom door being slowing opened drew her attention, she turned her watery face toward Jason standing there. Jason's eyes moved from Monique's troubled face to the TV where Crystin had just lowered her breasts toward Jason's seemingly hungry mouth. Jason turned off the tape, sat next to Monique at the foot of the bed with his head shamefully lowered.

"I can explain," Jason said somberly.

Monique gazed at Jason with an emotional look that she had never felt. She was beyond hurt, beyond anger and beyond any words that Jason could possibly say to her. She threw his hand off of her as if it were poisonous, an infectious something that would plague her body. Jason sighed heavily as the bedroom door slammed behind Monique. There was no getting around him having to face another consequence of his actions. Yet, for the first time he was uneasy about this particular dilemma.

After ejecting the tape, Jason found Monique staring out of their bedroom window.

"Sweetheart," Jason said softly as he approached her from behind. "Baby," he continued after a no-response from her.

Jason placed one of his hands on her shoulder, Monique turned around so swiftly that tears from her face projected onto him.

"Please sit and let me explain," Jason begged.

"What is there to explain? You were getting freaky with some woman," Monique replied troubled.

Jason placed two fingers on her chin, turned her eyes toward his and asked, "Do you love me?"

All of Monique screamed, *What the fuck does that matter?* But, she managed to utter, "Times like these, I question myself why I do."

"Understood. Please trust the love that you have for me and believe me when I say that what's on that tape was only business."

Monique's "you've got to be kidding me" expression was so apparent that Jason nearly laughed at his own words. She left Jason sitting on the bed, went back to the private solitude at the window and tried to will away tears again.

"Is this how you conducted your detective work?" Monique asked with disdain. "They now require officers to have sex to crack a case?"

"Sweetheart, the last thing I did before I retired was to work on Alfredo's attack, right?"

So, was the non-verbal expression that Jason received from Monique.

"Well," Jason continued, "what you saw on the tape was a part of that investigation."

"You told me about your taking down and arresting Alfredo's attacker. What I don't understand is how having sex with someone that I think that I know can be a pre- or post-action of the attacker's demise."

"The making of the tape was purposely omitted from my police report and deliberately not revealed to you at that time. The truth is, on that particular night, I was on a mission, my own personal vendetta to bring to justice Alfredo's attacker. Little did I know that Crystin," Jason paused as Monique's eyes seemed to overflow with the mere mention of her name, "and the man that was shot were waiting for me in the back of the modified SUV. It turns out that Crystin was so hurt by me dumping her after you made me realize what I was doing, that she devised a plan to discredit me by putting our sex video on the Internet."

"No Jason," Monique snapped. "On tape, you look as though you were participating."

"At gunpoint, my arms and legs were tied. Then Crystin did what she needed to do to get the physical response from me. Duress or not, if I'm kissed, fondled, sucked on and caressed long enough, my body responds. Any man would," Jason stated defensively.

"Then why in hell's name did you ask her for a kiss?" Monique struck back.

"Monique," Jason replied, he looked her squarely into the eyes. "It was all an act that played on her emotions to have her to release my restraints."

"Her riding your dick was part of the act too?" Monique asked harshly. Jason felt and accepted the verbal smack in the face.

Jason's eyes darted diagonally, then back to Monique. "For her," Jason said, "I guess not. She believed the things that I told her about us being together. Besides, there was nothing that I could do. She worked me to a hard-on, inserted it into her with hopes of getting pregnant."

"This just keeps fucking getting better," Monique replied in disgust.

"Fearing that she would succeed in getting me to an orgasm, I fed her everything that her troubled heart wanted to hear. She believed enough bullshit of mine until she eventually untied one of my hands."

"Enough! Jason!" Monique screamed. "Enough. I do not wish to hear any more. Just tell me, with our so-called open relationship, why am I just now hearing about this today?"

Jason stood and joined her at the window. He held her at arm's length with a hand on each shoulder.

"My Lovely Monique, I am truly yours. It has been that way since I cried like a baby in your arms. But, know that I will never keep you abreast of everything that I do. It is just my nature. If or when that happens, my disclosure or diluted truth is not an action against you. For one, I believe that some things should be kept to oneself. It is what gives you and me our own identity. The tape thing was kept out of my police report to prevent the press from having a field day with the Mayor's wife's affair. I kept it from you to prevent the pain that you feel today, this very instant."

Monique gazed at Jason because of the sentiment his voice carried.

"From the bottom of my heart," Jason continued. "What you saw was an act. It meant nothing then, nor does it mean anything to me now. It was just another circumstance of my not following protocol."

Monique's tears had all but stopped. She wiped the remaining swells from her eyes.

"Let me ask you what you asked me," Monique said.

Jason nodded.

"Do you love me?" Monique questioned.

"Yes, with all of my heart."

"Then, understand that I'm going to need time with this. First she flaunts the affair in my face at your retirement celebration, now real proof of the affair has my emotions in shambles. Even when you told me about it because you were assigned to watch her, in my mind it wasn't real, only speculative. But, that," Monique said with her attention now on the VCR tape on the bed, "drives the nail home."

Jason had never liked disappointing a loved one, especially Monique, the person who has loved him for so long. Even with the steady stream of tears gone, a mighty anguish remained on Monique's face. Disappointed with himself and defeated by the pain he had caused Monique, Jason kissed her politely on the forehead and swallowed heavily.

"I'm so sorry that you had to find out about this. I meant to destroy the tape, but it slipped my mind. Take all the time you need. I'll be here. I love you."

As Jason left the bedroom, Monique wanted to call out for him, but the bitterness inside silenced her words. She turned and gazed out of the window again.

"Why do I love such a complicated man?" Monique asked herself.

EIGHTEEN

Caramel questioned Jason Junior about the talk with his mother. She was mainly interested in how Monique responded to the inquiry. She hadn't known the younger Jason for too long, but she was sensitive to his mood upon finding out about the tape.

"Your mother denied knowing about the tape," Caramel asked. "Didn't she?"

"Yes, she rebutted all knowledge with a nervous laugh. I know my mom," Jason spoke with concern. "She was intrigued with the news and the curiosity will drive her to get answers."

"I feel responsible because I mentioned the tape to you."

"All of this drama started with me knocking over the box in the first place."

"But," Caramel rebutted. "I have you overly concerned with your mom's being-well...well-being," Caramel corrected herself.

"Don't worry, Monique Clemens will be fine. Jason has had a hold on her for quite sometime."

"What does he do again?"

"Nothing. He, or I should say, they are wealthy, but he used to be a police detective."

"Whatever he does is working. All you have to do is look around and one automatically knows that somebody is getting paid."

"All I was told was, that they came into a large sum of money."

◆◆◆

The next morning, the good life served Monique well. When Jason got out of bed to prepare for the Sixteenth Precinct, she replaced Jason's warm body with his pillow and mumbled something about preparing him breakfast. Jason told her that he was up early enough to have the first cup of coffee at home and stop to get a breakfast sandwich.

As Jason descended the stairs heading for the kitchen, the aroma of freshly brewed coffee tantalized his senses. He realized that Monique had set the timer on the coffeemaker as she did most nights, so he could have his morning drink. His mouth watered as it did every morning for the addictive beverage. When he walked into the kitchen, Jason was as usual, bare-chested with a towel wrapped around his waist. He stopped in his tracks upon seeing the refrigerator door open.

Monique's in bed, he thought. Jason quickly glanced at the feet below the open door, noticed painted toenails and was about to greet Caramel when the refrigerator closed slowly. Caramel was too shocked and embarrassed to do anything but stand in place in her near nakedness. She was like a deer caught in a car's headlights. For a woman her size, the see-through teddy looked good on her. The garment was pink in color, faded pink, or a splash of pink. Jason couldn't determine how much pink was in the teddy; the only thing certain was that garment contained just enough color to keep it from being transparent. It was short and hung just below her womanhood. Jason thought that the junior had or was going to get a special treat. Jason also felt that it was no time to be bashful seeing her in all of her glory.

"I'm guessing that the chill from the refrigerator has your nipples hard," Jason stated casually.

It was then that Caramel ducked, hid her body behind the center aisle.

"I'm sorry," Caramel said. "This is the first time you've actually come down while the coffee was the freshest."

"So, it's you who's gotten into the pot first," Jason replied.

"Yep. I'd pour me a cup, grab a dash of milk from the fridge and escape back to my room."

"It's no big deal," Jason responded. "Other than the way you're dressed... or lack of."

Caramel watched the man before her in awe. She admitted mentally that a man at Jason's age had a certain sex appeal. She fought the need to recite something flirtatious.

"I like to feel sexy," Caramel stated with a certain comfort.

"That you are," Jason complimented.

Caramel blushed. She felt her neck getting warm. It was the tell-tale sign of arousal when a red band about three-quarters of an inch thick, as brilliant as one of Saturn's planetary rings, formed completely around her neck.

Caramel felt it coming on. "Thank you," she said, attempting to concentrate and not fall further into a forbidden desire. "I still have thirty more pounds to lose," she commented where she stood. "I'm not a woman who is sixty pounds overweight, lose half as I've done and become complacent with the amount lost. I'm not stopping until the fat lady sings."

"That's very admirable. I'm confident that you'll make your goal. But for now, I think we both need to dress more appropriately for our morning coffee. If Monique or Jason saw us, we'd have some explaining to do."

Caramel slipped and gave Jason a devilish smile. Jason acknowledged and ignored it. Caramel poured milk into her coffee and headed out of the kitchen.

"Oh," she commented while turning around. "It wasn't the chill of the refrigerator that turned on my high-beams. It was..." Caramel winked at Jason, then turned the corner.

Jason poured himself a huge cup of coffee, headed upstairs to get dressed and thought to himself that he still possessed the ability to pull women from ages eight to eighty-eight.

NINETEEN

Orth and South sat in a car down the street from Jason's house with a pair of binoculars. They waited for Jason like two lions studying and stalking its prey. They had been watching the house for several days, noted that Jason and Monique had the company of the younger Jason and Caramel.

South was actually on the cell phone detailing what he and North's next action would be. The caller had grown impatient and wanted a more devastating action than the note that was placed into Jason's mailbox. The caller desired pain and suffering for Jason and all around him. South assured the irritated caller that their plan would work.

"There he is," North said.

When Jason got a comfortable distance away, they started the tail of Jason's vehicle. They used the binoculars to stay safely undetected behind him. As Jason pulled into the Sixteenth Precinct's parking lot, South updated the caller on Jason's whereabouts.

"So, he took the bait," the caller said. "It's about fucking time. He'll spin his wheels trying to find out who killed his Captain. This is what I want you to do...skip that 'Act Two' that you talked about and devise a way to take his ass out."

"Understood," South stated. A second later, South heard a dial tone in his ear.

♦♦♦

It was a rather informal procedure to reinstate Jason on the force. With his track record, along with the police commissioner's belief that Jason was near Godly, a quick signature on paper and presto, Jason was back, with full rank and status. The only difference was that Jason's entire pay would be donated to the Alzheimer's Association. The decision was based on the fact that Jason's father had started showing early signs of the crippling disease, so he felt obligated to help the foundation. He had already made a large cash donation from his sudden wealth, but he felt he could do more.

Jason noticed the young new hotshot sitting at his decorated desk as he approached Detective Austin.

"I love the smell of this place," Jason said to Kevin.

"I would have thought that the fresh air would have brought you to your senses. You liking the aroma of sweaty men, I may have to keep tabs on you," Kevin joked.

"I'm fine in that respect. I wanted to come back and help with Frank's case. All I want to do is help. You continue to be the lead in the case."

"We can do it jointly," Kevin responded. "I doubt that the short time you've been away has made you less of the detective you are."

Jason smiled.

"Besides," Kevin continued, "I'm counting on your bizarre instincts to be a major factor in busting this case wide open."

"I appreciate your vote of confidence...so, where do we start?"

"We start with you knowing what I know. I have everything with this case in a folder on the Captain's desk. Feel free to scrutinize, examine and put your mind on everything there."

"Thank you. Anything new on the case?"

Kevin anticipated the question and had rehearsed his response a thousand times, yet he wasn't proud of what he had to tell.

"There are no new developments. Even a handsome reward for information to solicit an arrest hasn't produced squat."

"No worries, mate," Jason joked in his best Australian accent. "Frank's murderer will be caught. Even a perfect crime has its blemishes."

"Get cranking on the files. I'll get back to you shortly."

As Jason sat in Frank's chair, he realized that the view from the opposite side of the desk was eerie. He visualized himself sitting across from himself being scolded by his beloved Captain. He was saddened that most of their communications were a direct result of his antics, a strong verbal lashing for something he did or did not do. Jason exchanged seats, sat in the one that he was more accustomed to. Oddly, he almost felt Frank's presence. He sat staring at the empty Captain's chair, found himself comparing the similarities between him and Captain North against him and his father.

With Frank, most of their dialogue was surrounded around the cases he worked on. With his father, most of their talks happened while they played dominoes. That was until the Alzheimer's disease made it too painful for his father to struggle with the numbers on the bones.

"I heard you were back," the voice of Detective McAllister came from behind him. "Are you okay?"

Jason was rather touched by Chris's concern.

"Even though I drove the man crazy," Jason replied, "Frank was like a father to me."

"Obviously, Frank thought of you as his son the way he covered for your ass."

"As I said, at times I know I drove him to drink. Hey," Jason stated with a conversation change, "what happened with Michael Jenkins?"

"Well, he is an ex-con convicted of armed robbery, but has paid his dues to society."

Jason found a great irony in the knowledge of Michael's car being stolen.

"He turned his life around," Chris continued. "He is married, but was seduced by the flesh of a hot woman named Toni Smalls. According to Michael, he followed her home, had sex with her and was knocked unconscious shortly after the act. He lost his credit cards, money and an expensive car when the woman's place was burglarized."

"What's the woman's take on this?"

"That's just it. After getting the address where the taxi company picked up Michael, we went there but no one answered the door. I got a subpoena the next day, entered the place but it was wiped clean."

"What! This sounds very fishy now."

"I know. Whoever was there did a thorough job of leaving no traces, no prints or DNA that an ultraviolet light could pick up. Everything, the apartment, the phone, and the furnishings were obtained with false information. You'd think with today's technology, that we would be able to trace something back to the origin."

"Understand that criminals nowadays have a better knowledge of the technology than we do."

"I know because, I'm stuck in one continuous loop. The description of the woman from one of the neighbors vaguely matched Michael's."

"These people are definitely pros."

"Indeed."

"And the brand on Michael's hand?" Jason asked.

"Just because you're in Frank's office, don't think that I have to report to you," Chris joked.

"It's not that, I've missed this stuff. Hearing the details of your case will help me regain my old karma."

"You're a strange man...anyway, we're looking into it. However, that part of the investigation is being kept on the down-low. I have a statewide probe going, looking for all heavyset officers with a limp."

"Great progress. You'll find out what's going on. I'm sure of it."

Chris didn't express it, but having Jason compliment him gave him a sense of pride.

"Detective McAllister," Jason stated. His professional tone caught Chris somewhat off guard. "What am I about to ask you?"

Relieved, Chris sighed and successfully replicated Jason's thought pattern. "You want to know about the limp." Jason smiled because of Chris's intuition.

"The neighbor," Jason stated to Chris.

"Yes," Chris continued. "She had no other physical description of a man visiting the apartment other than a limp."

"Often times, we get injured in the line of duty. There could be hundreds of officers in this city alone that might have that condition."

"I know," Chris concurred. "So, any progress with Frank's case?"

"Kevin basically told me that it was at a standstill. I haven't looked at anything yet," Jason said. His eyes peered at the various reports on the desk as if he, Clark Kent, was using his superior vision to review them. "I hadn't expected to be moved by simply walking into the office."

Jason stood, sat back in the Captain's chair as a gesture to Chris that it was time to get down to business. As if it were a secret code, Chris nodded and stated, "Do your thing."

Chris walked away without saying another word, nor did he receive a response from Jason. He hadn't expected one.

There were two stacks of folders piled neatly on the desk. One pile contained the coroner's report that detailed Frank's autopsy and the forensic reports on all of the evidence obtained outside Jazzpers. The other pile was the eyewitness accounts from the patrons of the restaurant. Jason's mind literally thought, *Eenie, meenie, miney, mo*, as he contemplated the starting stack. His hands hovered over a pile respectively with his eyes closed. Jason concentrated and hoped for a spark to determine which pile to start with. Consequently, when he opened his eyes, he noticed line one on the multi-line telephone blinking. He thanked God for the heavenly intervention and pulled the folders on the left toward him.

Even though Jason read both the coroner's report and the forensic reports slowly and methodically, he found nothing earth-shattering except the information about the fracture in Frank's skull. The coroner's report detailed that Frank suffered a head trauma. Jason's peripheral vision picked up the blinking light of line two on the telephone. The mild distraction gave him a sense of awareness, as did a unique sound of footsteps among many that he visualized coming toward the Captain's office.

"Monique is on line two," Kevin spoke.

"Thanks."

Jason separated the stack of folders with his hands as if he were dividing the Red Sea. He moved the piles to the left and right respectively to make room for his feet, which he propped on the desk.

"Hello, Angel," Jason greeted with an abundance of joy. "The mother of my child."

Silence greeted Jason's ears.

"Holy shit! I'll make it next time," Jason apologized.

"You'd better. You promised to be with me at most of my doctor's appointments. You're starting off a little shaky by missing the first one," Monique joked, but had a bit of seriousness in her tone.

"You can spank me later," Jason responded back.

Monique understood Jason's tactic. She was aware that he was refraining from discussing his return to the force for her benefit. She wasn't exactly happy about Jason's reinstatement, but she was pleased that Jason spared her the explanation.

"You'd like me to spank you, wouldn't you?"

"Now you're trying to involve me in your kinkiness. How did it go?"

"Things are normal. I had a sonogram today and I still can't get used to the chill of the gel that was rubbed on my stomach. Our baby is fine. However, at my age, the first trimester is a delicate one. My, or should I say, our next appointment is three weeks from now. I'll have to take the amniocentesis test during that visit."

"I'll be with you. You have my word," Jason promised.

"I do have some news that you'll surely find interesting," Monique replied.

"You know the sex of our child," Jason guessed.

"Not that, even though I was asked if I wanted to know. I'd rather be surprised."

"That's like you."

"My doctor gave me a few words of caution about having sex. Or as he put it, stay away from strenuous sex."

"You make me sound wild."

"That's because you are, nasty man."

"Nasty yes, wild I'm not."

"My dearest love, it is hard to be nasty without being a little edgy."

"Traditional it is. I wouldn't want to jeopardize our baby. Should your age be the determining factor that makes us refrain completely?"

"That's how I came up with the no-strenuous sex comment. I asked the doctor that same question."

"Again, if abstinence keeps our baby safe, I can wait."

"I know, sweetheart," Monique responded. "We'll be fine as long as we take it easy."

"Hey," Jason said with excitement. "I'm planning a special evening for you. It's my celebration to your upcoming motherhood."

"Strange, definitely strange, celebrating our pregnancy. It's sweet, but not necessary."

"It is necessary," Jason countered strongly.

"Hmm, I've learned that when you use that tone, it's best to say thank you."

"I promise. You will enjoy it."

"And, when will I enjoy this, 'it'?" Monique asked.

"Give me a day or so to get things in order. It takes a lot of coordination. As soon as I finalize things, you'll know. So, where are you headed now?"

"I'm dropping by Jazzpers. I hear they make a mean manicotti. The French martinis there aren't bad either." There was an uncomfortable silence from Jason's end. "And before you say anything, one drink isn't going to harm our baby."

"You know better than me. I will try to join you. First I want to get through most of these folders. It appears I have a lot of catching up to do."

"What am I about to say?" Monique asked.

Jason smiled. He knew his fiancée equally as well.

"Handle my business," Jason commented positively.

Even though you know we aren't in total agreement about this, Jason added for good measure, but only as a mental thought.

"I'll see you at home later," Monique said.

"Love you," their great minds spoke together.

Jason placed the telephone back in the cradle. Monique ended the call and used her free hand to rub her belly. She wasn't showing thus far, nor feeling any baby movements. She simply wanted to show their creation love at an early stage.

"Your Poppi loves you too," Monique spoke aloud.

TWENTY

Jason Jr.'s youth afforded him the strength to have a full-fledged sex-bout with Caramel, have enough energy to shower and leave for a grueling round of golf. Caramel found herself reminiscing about Jason Jr.; more precisely, she revisited the things he had done to her. Her body glistened with sweat even though her breathing had returned to normal. She was lying on the bed sniffing the wet-spot they had created. Her experience this time with the youthful Jason was far better than she remembered it to be on the island.

Caramel closed her eyes, tried to dive back into the exact sensation that wowed her when she released juices twice onto Jason's strong pole. Everything about her remained electrified, especially the tingle between her legs. Her hand crept down her silky stomach. Beads of water covered her baby oil-lavished body.

"Oh Jason," Caramel moaned when she inserted her middle finger into her moist-box.

She pushed against her jerking hips and found the sensation pleasing if not virtually erotic. As a vision of him played in her mind like a short film, Caramel envisioned Jason standing at the refrigerator in the towel he wore. She somehow received the same degree of arousal now as then when Jason gazed back at her. His muscular chest turned her on well beyond any form of denial. She wished the middle finger that began making circular motions inside her haven, was the older Jason's tool inside of her.

Caramel's moans increased when the other middle finger attacked her clitoris. It synchronized with the other one caught in a continuous revolving motion inside her wetness, seemingly churning butter. She forced herself to contain the release that she had worked up. Caramel bit down hard on her bottom lip just before a violent roar was to leave her mouth.

Damn it, she thought.

For a quick second her climatic state was interrupted by the sound of, "Anyone home?"

But, her mind processed the voice as the Jason she was fantasizing about. She grabbed a pillow, hugged it tightly around her mouth as the other hand continued to please her pleasure.

Jason, she thought. The faint electrical impulse of the thought electrified all within her. The intense scream that she released into the pillow was like none before. She bucked her hips wildly in the air, screamed Jason's name as she became far too sensitive for her own finger. Caramel's breathing was extremely heavy. She struggled to regain precious air, but, upon hearing footsteps ascend the staircase, the pillow was again used as a silencer.

Jason didn't bother to check the bedrooms because the car that the younger Jason was using during his visit was missing from the driveway. He assumed that with no response, the house was empty. Jason placed each eyewitness account of Captain North's death on the bed in his bedroom. Seconds later, Jason's naked frame stood in the shower. A steady stream of water tantalized his back. He closed his eyes and made mental notes as to the things that he personally wanted to investigate. Each new thought started with the same motion. He would tilt his head back; his face gathered the energy of the pulsating stream from the shower massage. Jason turned around, faced the front wall and let the water run through his hair, down his face while getting lost in the water's warmth. Jason blocked all sounds but the steady rhythm of the pulsating water that massaged his head. He was lost, unaware of anything until he picked up Monique's fragrance prior to the water dissipating the scent of Monique's favorite perfume.

The arms that draped around him brought on a broad and wide smile as he turned, still under the captivity of what felt like one-thousand hands.

"That was a quick trip to Jazzpers," Jason said as he turned to face his loved one. "Holy shit!" he responded stunned. "What the fuck are you doing in my shower?" Jason asked Caramel.

"I'm doing what any red-blooded woman in my shoes would do, going after the real thing," Caramel responded like a dog in heat. "I want the real Jason, not some dreamed-up copy that mimics you."

"Have you lost your everlasting mind? Get out of here before I spank you like the child you are?"

"You know that you want this. I can tell by how your dick responded to my hands on you."

"You give yourself too much credit, child. I thought you were Monique."

"That may be true, but I still got a rise from you."

Jason was disgusted. "Just fucking leave," he demanded entirely frustrated.

Caramel lowered to her knees toward Jason's joystick. Jason jumped back quickly, too fast for his own good. The round shower controller caught him directly in the small of his back. The lightning-fast pain caused his knees to buckle, this positioned Jason's manhood directly at Caramel's eager mouth. Jason swatted Caramel's hand away swiftly with force.

"Don't deny yourself one of life's simple pleasures," Caramel said.

Jason snatched the shower curtain back and stepped out of the shower quickly. His hasty retreat was the culprit that caused his second wet foot to slide on the tile floor. Both of Jason's legs flew up in the air as if they were snatched from under him. He fell hard and landed heavily on his back with a loud smack.

"God damn it!" Jason yelled.

He lay there trying to gain his composure. Caramel believed that opportunity knocked. She was sure that Jason hadn't seriously injured himself and wasn't going to let the chance to pounce on him disappear. She was more careful as she stepped out of the shower with wet feet. Caramel straddled him at the waist, hoped to work him up again. She leaned forward, gave Jason somewhat of a successful kiss because Jason continued to be disoriented due to the fall.

She leaned back and began to fondle his tool. Two hands grabbed a fistful of Caramel's hair from behind. Monique pulled hard; she literally attempted to remove Caramel's head from her body. Caramel was shocked, stunned and surprised. All of this ignited her self-defense mechanisms; she kicked backward forcefully without being aware of the move. The deadly foot impacted directly in Monique's stomach. Monique grimaced in pain for a couple of minutes and then crawled out of the bathroom with only the strength of her elbows, reminiscent of a combat soldier eluding enemy fire.

Monique became less of a concern to Caramel. She was defeated and crawled out of the bathroom like a *Chicken-shit*, Caramel thought. Jason was still under the influence of the fall and was pretty much defeated too. He had no resistance to Caramel's mouth performing fellatio on him. Her specialty proved itself, Jason became erected.

Monique found strength to stand after she cleared the bathroom's entrance. Doing so, her stomach ached immediately and immensely with severe cramps. She was terrified with thoughts of losing her baby. Yet, she managed to reach her destination.

Caramel, all things considered, had moderate success with the quest to harden Jason. She positioned herself to slide her wetness onto his pole. The first shot Monique fired was a warning, designed to get Caramel's attention. Caramel jumped away from Jason, hands behind her on all fours. She saw Monique, witnessed her bent over in pain, saw the heavy stream of blood that ran down one of Monique's legs and experienced her own terrifying moment as she saw Monique concentrate to steady the pistol.

"This is for my baby!" Monique yelled.

"No, please...No!" Caramel screamed.

◆◆◆

Jason had dried himself from the shower and had a towel wrapped around his lower half. He sat at the foot of the bed, putting lotion on his face when he heard a woman's scream. The bottle of lotion traveled yards across the room, propelled by Jason's quick action. He grabbed his pistol from the nightstand. Jason tiptoed down the hall, listened carefully for another distraught sound.

Caramel's nude sweaty frame sat up in the bed with her heart racing and mind disillusioned. Somewhere between her hearing Jason's voice and waiting for him to pass the room toward his bedroom, she had fallen asleep. The self-induced orgasm that followed the intimacy with the younger Jason had taken its toll. The dramatic explosion heavily induced by thoughts of the older Jason knocked her out like the strongest natural herb might. She was asleep before Jason finished placing the folders out on his bed.

When she heard the hinges from the bedroom door being slowly opened, she pulled the sheet over her, covered her from the neck to her mid thigh. Jason hid the pistol behind his back and prayed that the weapon's weight would not loosen the knot in the towel.

"Was that you who screamed," Jason asked.

"Yes," Caramel responded. Not believing yet pleased with the sight of him.

"Are you okay?" Jason asked with concern.

"I'm fine. I had a terrifying nightmare."

"Imagine the surprise I got when I heard you scream. I didn't think anyone was here."

"I must have been asleep when you came in," Caramel lied.

Caramel sat up in the bed with the sheet covering her alluring parts. She fought the impulse to be careless with the material.

This is the second time I've seen this man half-naked, she thought. *And, I can't do a damn thing about it, can I?*

"Well, if you're okay," Jason stated as he backed away. "I'll let you reflect on your bad dream. Sometimes it's good to do that."

If you only knew, Caramel said to herself. "Thanks, maybe I do need to give my dream some consideration," she spoke.

"See you in a bit," Jason said, then closed the door behind him. He sensed that there was more to her story.

TWENTY ONE

Monique met Jason as he exited the front door. Based on what she was told earlier, she hadn't expected to find him home so soon.

"Fancy meeting you here," Monique joked.

"My coming home early was unexpected. The no-smoking laws don't necessarily apply to police stations, well, not to the Sixteenth Precinct at the moment."

"You're bothered by the cigar and cigarette smoke now?"

"I suppose during my absence, I've developed a dislike to them. What's more amazing is that I suddenly can't stand the scent of smoke in my clothes. So, I came home for a quick shower and change of clothes."

"I'd guess now that you're back on the force, adjusting to the smoke is something that you'll have to reacquaint yourself with," Monique replied, just short of being smart.

Jason, like any man in a serious relationship, knew when to pick a battle. He let Monique's comment pass without a rebuttal.

"So, where are you off to now?" Monique asked.

"I'm headed back to where you just left. I need to get close to the crime scene. I'm hoping that some small details jump out at me."

"Do you want company? I don't mind going back with you."

"Thanks, sweetheart, but I'm going to sit in the parking lot and read these reports," Jason commented as he patted the eyewitness account folders tucked under his arm.

"Go handle your business," Monique said before she kissed him politely on the lips.

"I will," Jason stated. He gave her a playful smack on the butt. "I won't be long."

"See you soon."

Jason started his car as Monique disappeared inside the house.

How forgetful of me, Jason thought.

He exited the car with it running, made a mad-dash back inside the house and found Monique in the kitchen. Monique gazed at him, puzzled by his sudden return. Without a word, Jason dropped to his knees in front of her, placed his arms around her waist and kissed her stomach. Jason gave Monique a tender hug from where he was, got up and left without a spoken word.

Monique shook her head as she began to rub her stomach. "I told you," she spoke to their child. "Your Poppi loves you."

Monique walked by the smaller guest bedroom that Caramel was staying in. The door was cracked. She tapped on the inside wall near the light switch.

"Caramel, where is my son?" Monique asked.

"At the links," Caramel spoke with a distant tone.

"You're going to have to get used to being alone for hours when you're involved with a golfer. What are you doing?" Monique asked upon noticing Caramel packing clothes in her larger suitcase.

Caramel looked at Monique for a quick moment, went back into the closet for more of her things, but she didn't respond.

"I thought it was agreed that you could stay longer," Monique stated confused.

"It was," Caramel stated somberly.

"Then why are you packing your clothes now?"

"Because, I've worn out my welcome."

"I don't understand," Monique said concerned. "Has either Jason made you feel unwanted here? Did you and Jason have a fight before he left to play golf?"

Caramel stared through Monique as she pondered how to respond to the inquiries.

"No. No fights. Your son and I made love before he left," Caramel spoke without thinking. "He doesn't even know that I'm leaving. But, I have to get out of here before he gets back because I don't have a better explanation for him either. Monique, I just need to go," she said with a shaky voice. Caramel's eyes welled with water, but the tears stood fast.

"Do you want to talk about it? Maybe that will keep you from doing something rash."

"Rash is warranted. I have a taxi coming to take me to the airport. I'm flying back to Puerto Rico in four hours."

"Please don't leave without talking to Jason first. He can be a very rational person. And, you owe it to my son to say your goodbye in person."

"Ms. Monique, I'm aware of that. I've fallen for him. Don't you think if I could face him, I would?" Caramel gazed at Monique as if she were in serious pain. Tears made their way down her face. "I just can't stay here one second longer."

Why, Monique thought. She was lost for words and didn't know what to make of Caramel's mood swing or the urgency to leave.

"Since I can't help you with girl-talk or convince you to stay until my son gets back, may I at least take you to the airport?" Monique asked. She hoped to find answers to Caramel's dilemma.

"You'd do that for me?" Caramel asked even more disturbed.

"Child, come here," Monique said. She gave the troubled guest a motherly hug. "I'll be waiting downstairs when you're ready. I'll take the liberty and cancel the taxi for you. Agreed?"

Caramel's shameful nod accepted both Monique's ride to the airport and her cancellation of the taxi. She sat on the bed and watched Monique leave the room. During the drive to the airport, Caramel was eerily quiet. The kind of silence that told Monique that whatever the deep-rooted issue Caramel suddenly faced, it was huge and disturbing. Monique pulled to the curb at Caramel's airline's baggage check-in. Monique received a look of sorrow from Caramel before she lowered her head and stared in her lap.

"Please tell your son that I'm sorry and to please accept my call later," Caramel stated without looking at Monique.

Monique lifted the smaller of the two pieces of luggage from the trunk and placed it on the curb.

"It's not too late to turn around," Monique suggested.

"I know, but it's best that I go."

"As you wish, please keep in touch," Monique reluctantly conceded. "Just remember, you and my son have something special."

A friendly but emotional embrace was exchanged between the two women. Caramel separately walked each piece of her luggage to the skycap. Monique noticed a slight reluctance, but remained quiet.

"Ms. Monique," Caramel spoke. "Thanks for everything."

"No problem at all," Monique replied. "You are welcome here anytime."

"You know," Caramel stated before a heavy sigh, "when I was in my late teens, my mother told me something that I didn't completely grasp until visiting your home this past week."

Monique's brow rose as she waited for Caramel to explain herself.

"She told me," Caramel continued as tears fell from her eyes, "there was only room for one woman in her house."

Monique's expression showed enlightenment. As if Caramel stated a gender specific code, Monique understood Caramel's decision to leave her home. Even so, Monique's head nodded in wonderment. Caramel nodded back to signify that she was aware of Monique understanding. Caramel turned and walked away without uttering another word. Monique fought off the demonic thoughts of what may have transpired between Caramel and her Jason during the ride home.

TWENTY TWO

By the time Jason reached Jazzpers' parking lot, several phone calls had been made related to the extravaganza he wanted to plan for Monique. He felt great about what he'd accomplished in such a short time. Turning off the ignition was the switch to change thought patterns, Jason's mind went into full investigative mode. He started the investigation with a quirkiness of his personality which directed him to park his car in the very same spot where Captain North was murdered. When he stepped out of the vehicle, the first thing that he noticed was the burnt pavement caused by the massive fire. Burnt paint and a carbon stain still remained on the light pole.

Jason glanced at the Jazzpers building and tried to envision what the witnesses saw. He seemed to sense the fright and terror that some had experienced while they watched the raging fire. His eyes turned again to the charred pavement where Jason found comfort in knowing that Frank didn't suffer long. Jason sat back behind the wheel; attempted to block out the sounds around him as he began reading the first eyewitness report. Upon finishing, Jason realized that the other reports most likely wouldn't contain any useful information other than Frank's car being a bonfire. The second report mirrored the first one as did the third and forth report.

Jason's sensitive ears heard a car door shut from a distance. It was someone at the bank across the street. As he read the fifth, sixth and seventh reports, the identical thing occurred as it did while he read the second report. His concentration was broken by a car door and each time a person approached the bank's ATM. Jason stared blankly at the bank for a few moments, threw the remaining folders onto the opposite seat and then called himself a "dumb-ass." Soon, Jason sat at the light to exit Jazzpers' parking lot, jotted down another note and headed home to piece things together because part of the information he'd request would be best obtained during normal business hours.

♦♦♦

The next morning, a good many minutes before the bank opened, Jason sat in the bank parking lot staring down Jazzpers across the street. The irony was that the Bank of America organization was the company Sasha used to work for. It was her bank, the exact location of where she worked. Jason had no clue as to who replaced her as bank manager, but he was positive that her name could assist in his quest for information if needed. The amount of cars in the parking lot doubled when a vehicle parked three spaces away from him. The man gave Jason a curious glance as he walked by, and then proceeded to unlock the bank's entrance doors.

A moment later, Jason stood at the entrance. He watched the man disengage the alarm system.

"May I help you?" the man asked after hearing Jason's glass tap for his attention.

Jason held up his badge. "I need to ask you a few questions."

The man entered the small foyer between the first and second set of double doors where the inside ATM was located and spoke to Jason through the glass of the outside doors.

"What is this about?" the man asked.

"Murder," Jason replied bluntly.

Ben then unlocked the door and invited Jason inside. Ben was a man in his early thirties; he was professional, courteous and well groomed at all times.

"Thank you," Jason said as he entered the bank. "I'll be brief. I'm Detective Jason Jerrard. I believe you or your bank may hold information that can assist in a murder investigation."

Ben threw Jason another curious expression. "I'll help if I can, but I know there haven't been any murders inside this bank."

"That's just it. The murder I'm investigating happened outside."

"On bank grounds?" Ben asked excitedly.

"It occurred across the street in Jazzpers' parking lot."

"Wait a minute!" Ben responded even more animated. "Are you referring to the murder of the off-duty police officer a few days ago?"

"Yes."

"Now that I know what you're investigating, I still don't see how I'll be able to help you."

"Answer this for me. How often do you change the tapes in the ATM that faces the street?"

"They are changed every twenty-four hours and are on a thirty-day rotation."

"Perfect. I'd like to see the one from eight days ago."

As if a lightning bolt had struck Ben, he asked, "Jason Jerrard, Sixteenth Precinct? As in the Jason Jerrard who dated Sasha Fong?"

Jason was taken a bit by surprise by Ben's question, yet he managed to answer honestly.

"Yes, I was deeply involved with her."

"Oh my, it's definitely a small world," Ben said a bit surprised. "Sasha often spoke highly of you."

"I loved her too," Jason spoke somberly. "Parts of me still do." Jason shook his head as if the movement would place his thoughts back in order. "The ATM tapes?"

"I'm so sorry. I'm not trying to bring back the pain of old memories, I'm just happy to finally meet the person who brought her so much joy."

It was then that Ben realized he had not gotten over Sasha's passing. He began to feel troubled because Jason appeared to be dealing with the loss maturely and he didn't want his shortcomings to upset Jason's peace.

"Apologies," Ben stated without an explanation. "I'm happy to help. As I said, we keep each tape for a month and if you only need the one from eight days ago, then that one has not been overwritten."

"That's great news. It may hold information that could help my case."

"Give me a moment," Ben stated. He started flipping through the numerous keys on a key ring. He located the correct key to the ATM closet by the time he reached the door. "Will a copy of the tape work for you?" Ben asked from inside the small room.

"It would be perfect," Jason responded.

"I'd like you to know that I hated my promotion to bank manager because of Sasha's misfortune," Ben explained to Jason.

"Sometimes life presents us with situations like that. We must acknowledge when things are out of our control. Besides," Jason said more positively, "you got promoted because you're the best man for the job. Understand that if you walked away from this job, today or tomorrow, someone else would be running the show in your place."

"You are right. Corporate America is like that. Here you are," Ben stated as he exited the room. "I hope it helps."

"Thank you greatly for your cooperation."

"Anything for the person who made Sasha feel so wonderful. She glowed when she talked about you."

Jason hadn't forgotten about Sasha. He felt she would forever remain in his heart. However, Ben's constant conversation of her was uncomfortable to him. As if Sasha's ghost was haunting him. He thanked Ben and headed to the station to request information from the Virginia Department of Transportation.

Jason sat at Captain North's desk and summoned Detective Austin in his take-charge mode. Jason informed Kevin that he had a VCR tape from the bank's ATM. He also advised that he had requested visual representations from the four traffic-monitoring cameras at the light on Sixth and Maple streets.

"Very good thinking, Jas," Kevin said. "I'm sure something will come out of it. When can we expect VDOT's information?"

"I'm told I'll have it no later than next Tuesday. They are sending us four DVD's, one from each view of the traffic-monitoring cameras. So, I'd like you and I to view them together then," Jason suggested.

"Agreed."

"This way I can get peacefully through my big weekend."

Kevin smiled.

TWENTY THREE

The following Friday, Monique noticed Jason being fidgety. She had never seen him so out of kilter before over one of their dates. It was almost seven p.m. when Jason and Monique left Virginia City, took the shorter George Washington Parkway route toward Washington, D.C. to begin the special evening.

"How long are you going to keep me in the dark?" Monique asked during the ride.

"There is darkness involved for you tonight, but be assured that it will be worth the wait."

"Think so?"

"Know so," Jason answered quickly.

When Jason parked his car next to the nightspot called Zanzibar on Water Street, Monique instinctively knew that the dinner boat, "Spirit of Washington," was key in tonight's activity because the Zanzibar, though well known, wasn't diverse enough for his taste.

A romantic boat ride, Monique thought.

Jason accepted Monique's "I know what you're planning expression" because what he had in store for her was far beyond Monique's wildest dreams. Normally the "Spirit of Washington" would be open to the public for dinner cruises up and down the Potomac River, but tonight Jason had reserved the entire vessel for just him and Monique. They stepped onto the boat via a plank that was centered between the aft and stern of the vessel. They were greeted by the ship's Captain and the skeleton crew stood on each side of him.

After small introductions, the Captain escorted the couple to the stern section for their dining experience and entertainment.

"Where's everyone?" Monique asked.

"We are all here," Jason responded. "Just you and me."

Monique saw a lone table for two located on the edge of the small-sized dance floor. The table had a red silk tablecloth that nearly reached the floor on all sides. The table was covered with rose petals of various colors. Securing the colorful arrangement was a glass tabletop. A three-tier candleholder centered on the tabletop burned scented candles. There were two chairs, one for each of them respectively, but Monique noted that there were three table settings. Their plates had a decorative fan-folded cloth napkin and the third plate had a rectangular box sitting on it.

"Will you tell me what's going on now?" Monique asked as Jason pulled a chair out for her to sit.

"Yes, we are about to dine on the most fabulous food you've ever tasted," Jason replied. "You can order anything you want. I have truly covered anything that your heart desires."

A server approached their table, showed Jason a chilled bottle of champagne; Jason nodded in acceptance. As if the server was in an upscale restaurant, he poured over his elbow the sparkling beverage into the two tall crystal glasses on the table. Jason felt the server was being overly dramatic, yet he appreciated the gesture nonetheless.

"Aren't you a big spender?" Monique asked. "Cristal champagne tonight."

"I told you this is a special occasion for a very, very special lady," Jason spoke softly.

Monique was moved by Jason's words, but the added wink at the conclusion warmed her even more. She blushed and looked around to hide her face.

"What's on the menu?" Monique asked.

"In time, my love."

Outside, darkness had approached. Inside their section of the boat the lights were dim. Flickering candles in tall stands placed strategically throughout the room gave the setting a romantic flair. Their evening started with a violinist who came from behind a partition near the stage. She stood a few feet away and played a slow soothing, relaxing melody that neither Jason nor Monique recognized, yet they thoroughly enjoyed the selection. Monique smiled as her head began to sway to the feel-good music. The violinist backed away when she concluded her song. On queue, Rouel Martinezec approached them. He was the head chef at an exclusive restaurant in downtown Manhattan known for adding zest to any food.

"What can I prepare for the Madam?" the chef asked with a distinctive New Yorker accent.

"You're kidding, right?" Monique asked. "You are the menu?"

"To sum it up, one could say that," the chef responded. "I am equipped to prepare anything your heart or stomach fancies. Be assured, you'll have my robust twist to whatever dish you name. So, what will it be? Or shall I tantalize your taste buds with one of my specialties?"

Monique glanced at Jason, then shook her head as in stating "I don't believe you." She smiled, Jason received the "I love you" contained within. She pondered long and hard about the hundreds of possible meals that jumbled themselves in her mind.

Pick me, pick me, the various choices echoed in her thoughts.

Of all of the things that might appease her appetite, the last thing that Jason expected Monique to say was his meal.

"Eggs," she told the chef. "Runny eggs, bacon, toast, hash browns and grits," she finished excitedly. "Oh, and a pot of coffee placed on the table."

Jason's mouth opened in awe, yet it compared little to the shocked expression dawning his face. He somehow found amusement in the fact that he had spent thousands of dollars to fly a world-renowned chef down to personally prepare the meals and all that Monique wanted was breakfast food.

"Are you serious?" Jason asked.

"Very. I've always wanted to see what the appeal is with runny eggs."

"In that case," Jason said as he turned his attention to the chef who somehow managed to keep a straight face. "Double that order."

"Very well...runny eggs as in a little wet or a little soupy?" quested the chef.

Monique deferred the answer to Jason since he was the connoisseur of wet eggs.

"Soupy, definitely," Jason spoke.

"Coming right up," the chef responded.

The chef turned, walked away and thought, *Easy money*, although he was somewhat appalled that his talents were being wasted.

Monique saw several familiar sights of Washington, D.C. and Alexandria, Virginia as the boat traveled along the Potomac River.

"Fine champagne and eggs," Jason commented to Monique.

"Let's consider it a Mimosa without the orange juice," Monique joked.

Needless to say, Jason was impressed with the taste of their meal. It was simple, but his and Monique's palates were pleased sufficiently. Even Jason's runny eggs came out perfect. And, the zest given to the eggs for their distinctive taste was a hint of cinnamon.

The dinner-breakfast plates were removed; as they were served dessert, a six-piece band made up of three men and three women occupied the round stage.

"They are called Enchantment," Jason commented. "They are out of New York."

Jason had researched several bands that played a variety of tunes and was impressed with the rock, soul, hip-hop, big band, and jazz songs that Enchantment was capable of performing. One thing that finalized Jason's decision was the oldies video clips viewable on their web page. It truly displayed the band's enormous talent. The other thing that sealed the deal was their agreement to one special song.

"Good evening, Jason and Monique," the female headliner spoke.

"That's Myoshi," Jason boasted.

Myoshi was about five feet eleven inches tall with long curly black hair highlighted with brown tints. She had fair skin, slightly slanted eyes and a smile that could brighten the heavens.

They started a long melody of slow, soothing, piano and guitar tunes where Myoshi and the male headliner, Mike Hammond, swayed to the hypnotic tune. When Myoshi sang, Monique immediately became aware of Myoshi's demanding stage presence. But, her voice outshone any movement that her body could pose on stage. Myoshi sang the greatest love ballads from the sixties to present day with a powerful, smooth and enchanting voice.

Monique wanted to gaze at her man, but the aura of Myoshi's voice kept her eyes glued to the band like a fly trapped by flypaper.

"Do you like the band?" Jason asked Monique.

"Are you kidding? They are fantastic. Enchantment, why haven't I heard of them before?"

"At the moment, they aren't nationally known. They have actually performed for the King of Morocco. I'm confident that their big break will come soon."

"After listening to them, I have to agree."

"Does the lovely couple have any requests?" Myoshi asked.

Monique passed a gaze at Jason as she thought of a song appropriate for them. While Jason and Monique pondered songs, Myoshi and Mike walked off the stage with cordless microphones to the beginning melody of "Always," originally sung by the group Atlantic Starr. The singers greeted their opposite genders and serenaded each respectively until they reached the chorus of "I will love you so, for always." At this time, Myoshi and Mike would let the celebrating couple sing the sentimental line to each other. At the song's conclusion, Jason held Monique's hand tenderly. She was touched by the enduring words. Although they weren't originally his, her eyes filled with water and a lone wet tear trail moved down her face. Jason wiped the tear from her chin, stood and kissed his woman. After Jason's affectionate act ended, Monique was moved beyond words.

"I love you," Jason spoke heartfelt.

Jason extended this hand; Monique followed the invitation to stand and was led to the dance floor where a lone chair had been placed in the center. Jason kissed his loved one politely on the cheek, sat her and stepped behind her. The lights were lowered to near darkness. The oval windows on both sides of the vessel provided only a silhouette of the people moving about.

As the lights rose and the room illuminated, a melody of a song that Monique swore she had heard before played ever so lightly in the background. When the lights were returned to normal, Jason stood a few feet away in front of her. Jason sang the opening lyrics, "You remind me, I live in a shell. Safe from the past, doing okay, but not very well." When Jason sang the chorus, "And, I'm ready to take a chance again. Ready to put my love on the line with you," Monique recognized the decades-old Barry Manilow song.

Monique was awed. Jason had done lots of things to, for and with her, but sing to her was truly a first. She recalled that he hated the sound of his voice. She proudly watched her man, filled with emotion. As Jason began the next verse, he started a slow pace toward her. Timed perfectly, his arm extended just as he started the chorus again. Jason helped Monique to her feet and gave her an emotional hug. The band members finished the remainder of the song. They sang an extended version, repeated the chorus over and over at a lower volume while Jason and Monique danced slowly.

"You never cease to amaze me," Monique commented.

"And I hope I never will," Jason responded. "Do you trust me?"

"Yes," Monique replied. She lifted her head from his shoulder, then gazed at him with concern. "Why do you ask?"

"Continue to do so," Jason answered. "Please stay right here."

Jason went to the table, opened the rectangular box and returned to Monique. He placed the blindfold that was in the box securely around her eyes.

"What do you see?" Jason asked.

"Darkness."

"Good."

"Sweetheart," Monique commented with concern. "No forks today, please."

"No worries today, I'll use a knife," Jason spoke evenly.

Monique reached for the blindfold, but Jason caringly lowered her hand.

"Sweetheart, I was joking," Jason spoke softly in her ear.

As Jason walked Monique blindly by the hand, she sensed that the vessel was at a standstill.

"Jason," Monique called as she smelled fresh air. "What's going on in your diabolical mind?"

"Nothing. No matter what, trust me. You'll be okay. Go with whatever," Jason suggested as he released her hand.

Monique stood alone for a few seconds then felt a softer hand grab hers and lead her forward. She was guided to the other side of the vessel and was stopped immediately as the double doors closed behind her. The exterior windows of the thirty-foot walkway were covered for privacy. Candles on tall stands illuminated the enclosed area.

Monique was somewhat startled when she felt a hand at her ankles, but forced herself to find a sense of peace in Jason's words of trust. *A night to remember*, she thought.

"Lift your foot, please," Monique heard from below her. A shoe was removed. "Lift this foot," a different voice requested before the other shoe was removed.

Next Monique felt the zipper on her dress being lowered. *Trust*, she thought. In a quick moment, Monique was stripped naked. She was too embarrassed to speak, too trustful to fight what was happening to her. She was escorted for what Monique counted as three steps. Monique was instructed to lift her leg high and step forward. Monique complied and stepped into a circular bowl about ten inches tall and four feet of circumference. It had eight old-fashioned, cast-iron claw legs for support. Water with a silky feel covered her ankles.

Oh my God, she thought.

Monique strained her eyes to see what was happening, but Jason's blindfold prevented all but darkness. Her nose picked up the lily's fragrance that floated in the water. Monique was given a bath by what she believed to be two women with the softest loofahs that she had ever encountered. Blindfolded, foreign hands and the adventure of the unknown added a sense of eroticism to the cleansing. Afterward, she was escorted out of the bowl and dried with cushiony towels that had a springtime flowery aroma.

The undergarments placed on Monique were a matching laced bra and thong set.

Jason did his homework, she thought upon realizing that the bra fit her perfectly.

Monique believed she was a modern woman, yet she had never tried the newfangled butt-floss panties. Her sense of discomfort was just as she'd imagined it would be with the thong's material wedged between her butt cheeks. Monique's hands were raised above the head; she felt a dress being lowered onto her frame.

It's definitely not the one I had on, she thought immediately as the fabric touched her body.

The fabric felt different, so did the sleeves. She sensed that the garment hung higher above the knees, but when the garment was zipped in the back, the tighter feel was unexpected. She believed the garment to be far too heavy for lingerie and deemed it as a sexy dress that Jason had bought for her.

This dress better accent my girlish curves, Monique said to herself.

"Well," Monique spoke. "How do I look?"

"Beautiful," the two previous voices spoke.

"Almost there," a third voice spoke. "You're a true vision of loveliness."

The zipper was lowered and the dress was removed. Monique heard footsteps departing and a short moment later, the same sounding footsteps returned. This time when the dress was zipped up, Monique knew that the dress had been modified. The garment fit her snugly, but not as tight as before and it seemed to hang ever higher above the knees. Monique smiled because she had always known that Jason loved her shapely legs. The shoes she now wore were two inches taller than the previous ones. Then Monique's hair was brushed back to a style that was held in place by two small combs.

Monique was walked forward a few steps, then turned to the right and was instructed to step up. She stood in silence on a rectangular platform and heard footsteps circling her.

"That will do it," the third voice stated.

Monique's blindfold was removed just seconds before her mouth flapped open in shock. She stood in front of a full-length mirror. It reflected back the image of her wearing an off-white wedding dress. The two combs that held her hair back also supported a sheer veil that was pulled down over her face. Monique looked around and saw a woman that she'd seen before, but didn't directly know. The woman made an adjustment to one sleeve of the dress. The modification assured that both sleeves hung the same.

"Therez?" Monique questioned.

"In the flesh," Therez Fleetwood responded. "Hello, Monique. Your man is really something. He flew me in from New Jersey on short notice. Prior to that, he gave me everything to design your dress. He believed that the dress you're wearing is the one that you liked from my website. I made one minor adjustment and you'd think that your true measurements were taken."

Monique looked at herself in the mirror again and flashed back to one of her many visits to Therez's webpage.

CN004, Monique thought. "I'm in a wedding dress," Monique said nervously while Therez affixed the wedding gown's train to it. "I'm in your dress number CN004. I'm getting married," she continued as tears descended from her eyes.

"That you are," Therez replied.

Monique was handed a silk cloth to dry her eyes. A saxophone instrumental version of "Ready To Take A Chance Again" played as Monique stepped through a swinging double-door. Monique became filled with emotions, overwhelmed with a deeper love when she saw her man. There stood Jason wearing the finest black tuxedo with his hand extended.

"I'm ready to take a chance again," Jason spoke. "Are you?"

"Yes!" Monique yelled the joyous reply.

Applause came from the invited few that included Alfredo and Delia, Jason Jr., Detective Kevin Austin and the band members. Jason escorted Monique to a huge cross that had a kneeling bench in front of it.

"My love," Jason whispered. "I wanted us to kneel, but your dress is too short for that. I wouldn't want you being the cause of the minister pitching a tent," Jason joked.

Monique gazed at him in awe for a moment; mainly because of the surprise wedding and partially because Jason's humor escaped her. Suddenly, she found herself holding back her laughter.

He doesn't want me to give the minister a hard-on, Monique thought as she chuckled inside.

"This is no time to be funny," Monique spoke softly. "Kneeling, standing or rotating on our heads, I'll still marry you."

"This couple," the minister said as he addressed the attendees, "have already devoted their eternal love for each other in another ceremony, therefore, this will go down as the briefest ceremony in wedding history." He spoke to Jason and Monique, "Do you take each other lawfully, as husband and wife?"

A sentimental gaze was shared between the marrying couple. "I do," they spoke together.

"By the power vested in me, I now pronounce you man and wife."

After Jason kissed his new wife, he stated, "God is good all of the time."

"And all of the time, God is good," Monique said on cue.

TWENTY-THREE

Two days had passed since Jason's wedding. Two days since his bliss and two days since the bleakness. Jason sat at his home still wearing the tuxedo from days past. He had a massive hangover because of the alcohol binge he had divulged in since the momentous occasion. Jason wasn't relieved of duty. He had just refused to show up for work. He had isolated himself from the outside world. He had refused to answer the phone or door and had refused his body food.

He was unshaven, reeked of odor and still had nightmares about the event in his awakened state. He recalled the moments before his heart was ripped from his body seemingly with a jagged edged knife, but it was a single bullet. He remembered how magnificent he felt after being pronounced man and wife. He reminisced how passionate Monique's kiss felt as his wife. He remembered hearing what he thought was a champagne cork pop during their kiss, glass shattering and the sound the bullet made as it entered Monique's skull. He recalled how Monique's body collapsed when it fell limp in his embrace. The spray of blood that splattered onto his face would forever feel as though he'd been spat on.

Jason's scream when Monique's body went lifeless continued to vibrate through his body days later. No words described the pain and anguish that Jason was going through. He felt as though he was losing his mind. He had voices in his head and a vivid picture of Monique's eyes just after she received the deadly bullet. He couldn't shake the vision of how wide her eyes became. He remembered them looking like her eyes were being pushed from the inside, yet they contained an emotion of shock and sorrow.

Jason hadn't slept. He was exhausted to the point of hallucinations. Something had to give before he gave in to a depression that would consume, never release him and complete the path of self-destruction.

The night of Monique's death, her son immediately developed a hatred for Jason. As Jason sat on the boats floor with his dead wife's body cradled in his arms, the younger Jason ran over and threw a fury of punches at him. Jason simply held his new bride tighter and accepted the array of punches without any reprisal. Kevin Austin came to Jason's rescue and wrestled the enraged son to the floor. The younger Jason believed with every fiber of his being that Jason was directly responsible for his mom's death. And, in the back of his mind, he believed Caramel's departure had something to do with him as well.

Monique's son's emotionally troubled question to Jason was one of the many twisted thoughts that began to drive him mad.

Why wasn't there a second shot at you? The daunting question ran through his mind.

Jason was about to pour himself another tall serving of straight Cognac. With his arm extended, ready to pour the forget-all nectar, two things happened simultaneously. He smelled his underarm stench. Never mind the fact that the bottle was empty. This released the thought that something must be done about it. Then under all of the stimulants that he had consumed, the answer to Monique's son's question nagged him.

"I don't know why a second shot wasn't fired at me," Jason spoke as if Jason Jr. were present.

After minutes of repeatedly asking himself the question, "Why a second bullet wasn't fired?" an enlightening revelation occurred. *The bullet wasn't meant for me*, he thought.

"I wasn't the fucking target!" Jason yelled as if Monique's son could hear him.

Jason leaned back against the sofa, arms initially spread across the sofa's back. That was until the odor from both underarms forced his arms to the side. Jason began to get angry with himself for being in his current state. He believed that if he hadn't tried to drink away the sorrow, the question about the second bullet would have been thoroughly thought through much earlier. When he stood, his head pounded heavily because of the drinking spree and the lack of coffee.

First things first, Jason thought. *I need to brush my teeth and rid myself of my fucking funk*.

After a rather disturbing trip to the bathroom where he witnessed first-hand how awful he looked, Jason stood in the kitchen with his tuxedo jacket removed, shirt unbuttoned and pulled out of the pants; he filled a glass coffee pot with water. Jason sighed just after filling the brewer with water because the doorbell rang a second time.

Jason stared in the direction of the sound. Six, seven, eight times in rapid succession the doorbell chime sounded. As if the person was a fly hovering on and around manure, Alfredo was persistent with the doorbell button. Alfredo's diligence was as annoying as fingernails being scraped across a chalkboard until Jason started for the door to swat the pesky insect.

Jason was relieved that it was Alfredo; he felt as though he couldn't bear any other person's company. He invited Alfredo in without a word, made his way back to the kitchen and watched his dear friend begin picking up the various empty alcohol bottles scattered here and there.

"Coffee?" Jason nonchalantly asked.

"One, two, three," Alfredo counted as he dropped the bottles into the trashcan.

There were five empty bottles in all, whiskey, vodka, gin and not to mention the half-bottle of Cognac sitting on the living room table.

"No thanks," Alfredo replied. "You can die from this shit. Ever heard of alcohol poisoning?" Alfredo asked sarcastically.

Jason gazed at his friend with as much shock as his mental and physical state would allow. He realized that it was the first time he'd ever heard a foul word spoken from Alfredo's mouth. Alfredo stared back while shaking his head from side to side. His eyes displayed an abundance of dejection with Jason's appearance and the condition of his home.

"Water, if you have bottled," Alfredo continued.

"I'm okay," Jason told Alfredo. He lacked anything better to say.

"Yes you are...or you will be. I dropped by to give you the kick in the butt that you so desperately need. Everyone has tried to contact you. Your voice-mail on both the home and cell phone is full and not accepting messages."

"I just needed time to reflect," Jason commented in his defense.

"Jason, my dear friend. That's bullshit!"

Again, Jason looked at Alfredo as if he were another person. Profanity twice in less than five minutes was like a revelation for Alfredo. The comment, however, told Jason that he wasn't taking any excuses, nor was Alfredo willing to let Jason drown in self-pity any further.

"I know I cursed. Don't be surprised; when time warrants it, it will be stated without hesitation. And, this is definitely one of those times. You need to get a strong grip on yourself, my friend."

"My wife was murdered in my arms. Can I have some leeway to grieve?"

"What you've done for the past few days is not grieve. You've shown signs of giving in. The great Jason Jerrard wallows in self-doubt."

Jason regarded his dearest friend in a manner that spoke volumes. Alfredo felt every curse word and ill thought that passed through Jason's mind. Yet, he stood fast and didn't back down from Jason's silent aggression.

"All of the people I care about get hurt," Jason spoke somberly. "You, Sasha and now Monique. Even Monique's son has abandoned me."

"You'll fix things with him as soon as you fix things with you. Your healing starts by first understanding that Monique's death was not your fault. You are not to blame."

Jason felt a wave of emotions sweep him.

"I believe," Jason said, despite Alfredo's words, "the deadly bullet that killed Monique wasn't meant for me. So, Monique's association with me caused her death. She became a victim of my circumstance," Jason spoke with trembled words.

"She became a victim of life," Alfredo responded. He wasn't trying to sound cold and uncaring. He simply spoke a fact.

"That's all and that's all it will ever be," Alfredo continued. "The person who shot her wanted to send you to the very place that you're in now. And from my perspective, they have succeeded. My only question is...are you going to let them continue to win?"

Jason's mind was someplace foreign to Alfredo. Alfredo knew his words were being heard and he believed Jason's dead-man's stare was his internal way of coping with the harsh reality of the truth in Alfredo's words.

Jason finished his cup of coffee, and stood motionless for a moment because somewhere buried in the cloudy clarity of Alfredo's words, his heart spoke.

"I've loved her since high school," Jason announced unknowingly.

Alfredo put a hand on each of Jason's shoulders, looked him squarely in the eyes. "No one will question your love for her," Alfredo responded. "I know you do, God knows you do and most importantly, your heart knows and forever will. So don't dwell on that. My best piece of advice for you my dear friend is...you need to do what Jason would do."

"That Jason would cease the drama," Jason spoke. "And get his ass out there to find the person who was responsible for..."

Jason paused. He was uncharacteristically timid about mentioning Monique's death. He and Alfredo sat at the kitchen table. Alfredo regarded him with sympathy. He empathized with what Jason must be going through, yet he knew Jason was better than the condition of his current mental state. Therefore, his words to Jason had been more of a fatherly verbal lashing rather than a friend to another friend in need of a shoulder to cry on.

"Thanks for coming," Jason said. "I do appreciate your concern."

"You know how I feel about you. That's a given. I just want you to get back to you."

"I will," Jason responded not completely convinced of his own words. "My pity party is over."

Jason's positive words did little to combat the bitterness that flowed through him. But, a tiny spark told him that it was a start.

"You've had tons of people trying to reach you," Alfredo commented once more.

"I know. My telephone rang constantly until I finally took it off the hook. Be assured, my self-indulged hibernation is over."

"Then maybe you should start by removing the two envelopes taped to your front door."

"Oh?" Jason sounded surprised.

"You might have seen them if you had fully opened the door when you let me in. You turned and walked away so quickly I wasn't sure if I was welcome."

Jason excused himself. He looked at the disarray that the living room was in as he approached the front door. Immediately, Jason knew that the recognizable envelopes would represent another dismal chapter in his life. The envelopes were marked with the number two and three respectively on the exterior.

Jason snatched both envelopes from the door, closed it behind him and opened the lower numbered one first. As Jason read the first of the two enclosed notes, slowly he fell against the door and slid all of the way down to a squatting position. His head lowered, his heart abandoned its calmer state and became a heavy pounding instrument.

Compose yourself, Jason demanded his being. *Fight*.

Jason smacked his hand on the floor, steeled his emotions and rejoined Alfredo at the kitchen table. Jason's eyes had turned solemn. He passed Alfredo the paper that was enclosed in the envelope marked with the number 2 and opened the remaining one.

"Act Two – The Bullet," Alfredo read. Alfredo felt a sudden grief with what he read. He understood why Jason's facial expression was a deeper mixture of pain and anger when he returned.

"I suppose you don't know who typed this. Is there more?" Alfredo asked.

Jason closed his eyes, then sighed heavily before exhaling slowly.

"Yes, there's more trouble," Jason responded just sort of being enraged. "It seems that two more will die if I relate this in the manner that it relates to Monique's death," Jason commented while he passed the second paper to Alfredo. "I truly am not aware of who is fucking with me," Jason said as calmly as the internal anger would allow him.

"Act Three – The Third Body," Alfredo read this time.

"It reads as though more mayhem is coming your way," Alfredo said as a word of caution.

"My friend," Jason responded. "Maybe you should distance yourself from me. I'd hate for you to be the third body this warning talks about. Then again," Jason said as an afterthought, "I wonder who the second one might be."

Alfredo nodded. He understood Jason's concern.

"I'm going to follow the lead of the real Jason," Alfredo commented. "I'll be brave and not be intimidated by the unknown."

"Thank you. I get it. I'm going to get myself together...starting right now," Jason said as he stood.

Alfredo stood after him and gave Jason a man hug. The kind of hug that starts with a handshake, followed by collapsing elbows and a quick squeeze with the other arm around each other's shoulders.

"Handle your business," Alfredo told his friend.

Alfredo was unaware that Jason's "I will" response was a new resolve invoked by the identical words that Monique often spoke to him.

"Thanks again for coming to see me. Your," Jason thought for a quick second, "kick in my ass was much needed and well deserved. I feel your concern here," Jason said as he pounded a fist several times against his heart. "I got it. I know what I must do."

"Very well. Will we be seeing you at the restaurant later?"

"Count on it," Jason responded. "Count on it, my friend."

TWENTY FOUR

Jason cleaned himself up nicely. He put on the usual shirt and tie ensemble and then headed where his heart dreaded the most. Though externally, he appeared to be his old self; internally his emotions were as frail as rice paper. As he drove to Virginia City's morgue, the question, *Who did this?* played constantly in his mind. His steps through the morgue were slow and painful, multiplied tenfold by the recentness of viewing Captain North's body. It wasn't that he disbelieved Kevin about Frank's death; he just wanted to say a few words privately without the hoopla of a funeral.

However, with Monique it was different. He would have private words with her, but it would be the first time mentally that Jason would fully accept her passing without the liquid alcoholic stupor manifesting his grief into a depression. Jason held his breath as Monique's body was slowly pulled out of what he deemed as the refrigerator. He released his breath, gazed at her in silence and remembered her loveliness as she approached the cross on their wedding day. He recalled her being perfect in every way, almost Angelic; she seemed to float toward him. Jason grabbed one of her chilled hands just as a tear formed in his eyes.

"I'm so sorry," Jason said somberly. "I failed you. My lack of extreme concern with the first note caused this." Jason's head tilted backward, his eyes gazed toward the heavens. "I will always love you," Jason softly spoke.

His words opened the flood gates in his eyes. Jason felt the echo of his pounding heart vibrate in his ears. Suddenly, a deeper misery tried to consume him. His hand gradually moved toward Monique's stomach. He placed his hand with fingers spaced wide on her cold body and hoped that the warmth from his hand would bring back their lost baby.

Two loved ones lost, four people dead, ran through his mind. The thought alone made him want to hate his life, the world and the people in it. Instead, he directed the negative energy into a determination to let life happen to those who caused his pain.

"You are my love," Jason spoke aloud. "Now, I'll seek your revenge. Love and Justice is all that I'm about now. I will seek justice against those who took my love from me."

Jason held Monique's hand once more. He looked around at all of the similar doors that housed other lost souls. All cold, confined alone in darkness, much like his heart. He placed a tender hand on the side of Monique's face, leaned over and kissed her Popsicle-like lips. He wished his lungs could fill her lungs with a new life. He began praying as the chill of her lips coupled with the sudden realization that one of his fingers was touching the bullet hole in her head. These two things forced the reality of the situation, truly awakened him from this pipedream.

Before Jason left the morgue he arranged for the cremation of Monique's body per her request. He would return in three days to pick up the ashes.

TWENTY FIVE

Jason wished there was a usable rear entrance into the Sixteenth Precinct. Unlike walking into the morgue, Jason's pace was fast, filled with purpose. Jason's eyes stayed focused on one thing, the door to Captain North's office. He ignored the many glances and comments that came his way. When he closed the temporary office door, he felt a great deal of relief hiding in the false sanctuary. Jason sat at Frank's desk, then pulled from his bag the remaining folders that he had yet to read. He heard a quick knock, and then noticed the door being opened.

"I already know how you are because you didn't report to work or return any of my phone calls," Detective Austin spoke. "What I want you to know is... I'm personally handling Monique's case. I'd like you to continue with Frank's case."

Jason's thought of him being the senior detective over Kevin was never verbalized.

"You can handle that, can't you?" Kevin asked.

A half-smile formed on Jason's face. He knew that Kevin's straightforward manner wasn't a doubt of his ability to conduct Frank's case, even with his current mental condition. It was Kevin's indirect way of informing Jason not to get involved in Monique's investigation. An identical smile found Jason's face because he believed Kevin's indirect order was like asking a bear not to shit in the woods. However, Jason didn't offer a rebuttal.

"Understood," Jason simply responded.

Kevin took Jason's response very lightly. He appreciated the fact that

Jason didn't outwardly challenge the instruction. Kevin reminded Jason that Monique's investigation had his full attention and his best effort.

"I'm heading back to the waterfront," Kevin stated. "We will exchange details later. The Metropolitan Police have pretty much let us conduct the investigation."

Kevin turned and walked away before Jason could inquire about Monique's investigation. Jason felt that Kevin was fully capable of conducting her investigation, but staying away from her case would test his resolve. A test that he'd surely fail because no way, no how, was he going to do nothing for the one he loved. Jason did decide to wait until they exchanged details on their respective cases so he could determine the best angle of attack to snoop in Monique's case.

Jason sat idly for a moment. He reflected on all of the women he'd had in his life. Not the people who filled empty spaces and lonely times, but the ones whom he truly loved: Julie, Sasha and Monique. He tried not to dwell on the fact their deaths had one common factor, him. Another quick knock on the door occurred, followed by the door being opened disturbing Jason's destructive thoughts.

"Jason," an officer said. "I'm glad that you're back. You need to see this," the officer continued excitedly.

Jason was intrigued by the young officer's sense of urgency and puzzled why Michael Jenkins was standing next to the reporting officer.

"Chris is not around," the young officer said. "When he mentioned your name second, I thought I'd bring him to you."

"Thank you," Jason responded.

The officer nodded, stepped aside to let Michael enter the office and closed the door behind him when he left.

"Mr. Jenkins," Jason said. "Is everything okay with you?"

"I'm doing well. Thanks so much for the call to my parole officer. Because of your efforts, I only received a verbal reprimand for my involvement in the car incident. I can handle that."

"Good. It was my pleasure to help. So, what brings you here today?"

"Do you remember my brand?" Michael asked as he held up his bandaged hand.

"Yes I do. Your brand was what led us to believe a cop or ex-cop was the person who attacked you. Is it healing okay?"

"It's coming along nicely, but in the process, it has changed slightly. The more it heals, the more clarity it has. Before, because of the swelling only the larger letters were legible, but now, two more letters are clearly recognizable."

Jason stepped around the desk while Michael unwrapped his hand. Jason observed the change in Michael's cattle-like brand. He saw around the circle of the ring a letter, four numbers and another letter. He sat back behind the desk and stared blankly beyond Michael.

"I'd gather from your reaction that you know what the new information means," Michael said.

"Yes. I believe so."

Jason picked up the telephone and requested a member from the forensics team to come to the Captain's office. Michael looked at his hand closely, glanced at the nameplate on the desk; this produced an eerie feeling inside him.

"No way!" Michael spoke in disbelief.

"That's my gut feeling," Jason replied. "The four numbers represent the year he graduated from the academy and the two capital letters definitely stand for Frank North. Whoever branded you is my Captain's murderer or has a connection to the crime itself."

"Did anyone talk to the woman I was with? Whoever burglarized her home will be your killer."

"I was told that an attempt was made, but the place was empty and wiped clean."

"What!" Michael sounded astonished. "The place was filled with plenty of expensive furnishings."

"That's a strong indication that your robbery and the Captain's murder are connected. Now, with your brand being clearer, all suspicions have been justified."

Michael found the situation hard to believe. He was surprised that a woman who outwardly appeared genuine and trustworthy could be mixed up in a crime scheme. Jason began thanking Michael for coming back in when an officer from the forensics team entered the office.

"Carver," Jason spoke, "take Mr. Jenkins and retake photographs of his hand. It's definitely a link to Frank's murder. And, Michael, you're free to go when they are finished."

Michael nodded, said goodbye to Jason and left with Officer Carver. Jason remained in the seat. He thought, *find the woman and you'll find the man.*

TWENTY SIX

"How did it go?" the caller asked.

North responded, "Very well, you know how we do."

"Ah," South chimed in on the other phone. "We didn't exactly stop our three-act theme. I'm happy to report that Act II played out perfectly."

"What the fuck was Act II?" the caller yelled. "I told you to kill the mutherfucker."

"True," North spoke. "But, you also told us to make his ass suffer. Act II definitely accomplished that."

"Get to the fucking point," the caller responded annoyed.

"Well, we watched Jason board the Spirit of Washington at the marina on Water Street in D.C. We then snuck on this yacht a mile or so away down the Potomac River. We took care of the owner," North said seconds before bursting into an uncontrolled laughter. "We caught this dude in the head whacking his dick off. Anyway," North continued after he realized the humor was lost with the caller. "We then sailed down the Potomac and anchored fairly close to Jason's boat because surprisingly, they were anchored not far from where they started. When the opportunity presented itself, South shot his woman dead."

"Jason deals with death every day. He won't suffer because you killed someone he was fucking."

"I beg to differ," South jumped back in. "Apparently Jason had this elaborate evening planned aboard the Spirit of Washington and as luck would have it, she was in his arms. They were celebrating the post-wedding first dance and I took her away from him practically moments after they said 'I do.' I saw his reaction through the rifle's scope. Believe me when I say that the bastard was horrified."

"Wait a fucking minute," the caller interrupted animated. "The yacht explosion on the news was you guys' handiwork?"

"That's right. We used that so we could escape unnoticed."

"What did you do, walk on water like Jesus?"

North, South and the caller found the question humorous. After the laughter died, they reminded their partner that they were prolific swimmers. Therefore, with scuba gear, the approximate one-mile swim above and underwater back to where their car was parked was a mere technicality.

"So you see," North commented. "The timed ship explosion was the perfect diversion that guaranteed our escape, undetected."

"Where is Jason now?" the caller asked.

"Today, we followed him to the Sixteenth Precinct. Before that he hibernated in his crib like a little pussy. Several people dropped by since his wife's death, but he refused to answer the door. I'd say that's a real sign of suffering."

"Good. Good. I want to see both of you before you implement Act III," the caller suggested. "Shit, I have to go," the caller stated hurriedly. "See you guys soon."

TWENTY SEVEN

When Detective Austin walked into Frank's office, Jason had the telephone receiver at his ear. It was one of many attempts where Jason had tried to contact Monique's son. To no avail, Jason tried communicating with him via all available numbers. However, the younger Jason was coping with his mom's death in a way that best suited him. Monique's Jason had shut out of his life the man he once believed was damn near perfect and replaced the admiration with hatred. All based on a diluted belief that Jason was responsible for his mom's death.

Jason hung up the phone without leaving another message. He chose not to because he was sure Monique's son was either listening to or just simply deleting the messages. Otherwise, the younger Jason's voicemail would be full by now.

"Jas, I have the report back on all of the officers with a limp," Kevin spoke. "I filtered out the deceased ones and those out of the surrounding area. That leaves us with two active and two retired suspects "

"Thank you," Jason responded. "Anything else?"

Jason's question was derived to get Kevin talking about Monique's case, but after years of working with Jason, Kevin recognized Jason's tactical maneuver.

"Yeah," Kevin continued. "I put VDOT's DVD's in the same drawer where the bank's VCR tape was. Hopefully, they will produce a lead."

Jason looked at Kevin as though he had lost his mind. He was distraught that Kevin wouldn't divulge any information regarding Monique's case. Kevin turned and walked away. He felt bad about what he did, yet he understood that it was necessary to keep Jason focused on Frank's case.

"In time," Kevin stated as he closed the office door. "Give it time."

Jason took the VCR tape and the four DVD's to the sixth floor. He walked into the technology side of the forensics team area. The room housed some of the most advanced computers for image manipulation that dealt with the type of media that Jason had in his possession.

Jason solicited the assistance of Alexandra Thomas. Alex was the name she instructed people to call her. She was in her mid-thirties and was what people called a geek, all the way down to the tape on her square glasses. In college she had majored in computer science because of her fascination with electronics and graduated like Jason at the top of her Police Academy class. Stranger than the tape affixed to her glasses was her attractiveness; she happened to be the most attractive and alluring woman the Sixteenth Precinct had to offer, but the thirst for her profession kept her alone without a serious companion in her life.

"I'd like to be able to view and manipulate the images on these media," Jason told Alex.

"That should not be a problem. We have the ability to enhance, enlarge, cut and paste various media formats," she replied. "It all can be viewed on those two large monitors."

Jason followed her eyes to the dual plasma monitors directly in front of them mounted on the wall.

"Which one do you want to start with?"

Jason gave Alex the VCR tape. "This should have a view of Jazzpers' parking lot where Captain North was killed," Jason stated. "I'm hoping to at least determine the exact time Frank's car arrived in the parking lot."

"There is a time marker in the bottom right-hand corner of the tape. What time frame are you interested in?"

"I'm not sure. Let's fast-forward to the explosion and work our way back."

Even with numerous cars passing on the street and people utilizing the ATM, the bank's ATM camera provided a wide view of Jazzpers' parking lot. However, the picture quality was grainy, even with the enhancements from the computer's software. Once the video was at the explosion, Alex used the brightness from the flames to sharpen the picture quality the best she could.

"Now," Jason spoke, "reverse it slowly. Let's get back to when Frank's car was parked under the lamppost."

Jason couldn't make out the features, but he determined for sure the silhouette moving about before the explosion was Frank. The reverse play of the video back to when Frank's car was parked under the lamppost disturbed Jason. He acknowledged that Frank was dead, but what he observed made the situation all too real for him.

"Half-speed forward okay with you?" Alex asked.

"Fine, but can you magnify and just show the surrounding area of the car?"

"That's simple enough," Alex replied before negotiating a few more mouse clicks.

Jason ascertained that there were two people in Frank's car when it parked under the lamppost. He determined that a man was the driver based on the strength needed to move Frank's dead weight body into the driver's seat. Jason had Alex pause the video at the point where Poncho walked in front of the car.

"Can you enlarge that person?" Jason asked.

"Here goes," Alex stated as she isolated the image and then magnified it with a few mouse clicks. "Understand that even with the lamppost's illumination the bank's camera is just not strong enough to give you anything more than a very poor grainy picture from that range. Enlarging the image you'll only see more distortion than detail."

Alex's assessment proved to be correct to Jason's eyes.

"Damn," Jason cursed. "I was hoping to see some facial detail."

"Sorry, fuzzy silhouettes are the best I can do. The phrase, 'junk in, junk out' is appropriate for the quality of the VCR tape."

"I see that. Let it play," Jason instructed.

Jason was horrified as Frank's car exploded and burst into flames. The half-speed playback seemed as detailed as a frame-by-frame viewing would be. What was even more disturbing was the acknowledgment of Frank's movement prior to the raging flames.

"Look at that," Jason's anxiety forced him to speak excitedly. "He was conscious right there."

"That's awful that he woke up just in time to die. The poor soul never had a chance."

"Please rewind the tape back to the two people sitting in the car and play it back at full speed," Jason said.

While Jason watched the event unfold, time appeared to stand still. Oddly enough, Jason noticed something clearly undetected while viewing the tape at half-speed.

"Right there!" Jason spoke. "Rewind the tape back to when the man closes the passenger side door."

"I didn't see anything different than before," Alex replied fueled by Jason's excitement.

"Watch carefully as the man leaves the car and walks in front of the vehicle across the camera's view. The man...has...a?" Jason asked slowly.

"A limp," Alex spoke in conjunction with Jason.

"I can't believe," Alex said, "a man with such an attention-getting walk could just walk away without being noticed."

Jason watched the tape repeatedly. He hoped to discover another clue that would aid in identifying the person second on his personal most-wanted list. Jason saw the feeble attempt at dousing the flames by the establishment's manager, the fire trucks' arrival and the many patrons of Jazzpers that witnessed the spectacular bonfire event. What Jason didn't expect to see was the person with a limp come back into view and get into another vehicle after all of the hoopla diminished and people started dispersing.

"That has to be the same guy," Jason said when he noticed the familiar dip in the suspect's walk.

"I believe you're right," Alex concurred.

"Can you zoom in on the car's license plate?"

Alex gave it her best effort, but the amount of darkness combined with the distance the bank's camera lens had to travel didn't produce a glimmer of hope to decipher the license plate number.

Jason had Alex start the tape from the beginning and they watched the events unfold in silence. Jason had still pictures printed of the scenes that he deemed important. One of which he wanted to study closely was the best available in identifying the make of the car that the assailant got into.

"Would you like to take a break before we view VDOT's DVD's?" Jason asked.

"I'm holding up well. Besides, it may be best to simply let you handle your business."

Jason sighed heavily, fought against the depression that swept over him.

"As an afterthought," Jason said, "a cup of coffee would help me relax."

Alex gazed at him with puzzlement. She detected a slight mood swing although Jason tried to conceal it.

"I'll be back momentarily," Jason stated.

He left the room in an odd fashion. Several minutes later, Jason returned after visiting the mens room where he splashed water onto his face and slapped himself as if he needed to wake up. Alex couldn't disregard Jason's awful attempt to smile. Her head shook from side to side.

"I'm not privy to what happened a few minutes ago, but you looking at VDOT's DVD's would be a grave waste of time. Your focus is absent, blank like the expression on your face."

Jason became concerned about Alex's knowledge of his vanishing mood. After all, it was Alex's words that were familiar to him, the very same words spoken to him countless times by Monique. But, he couldn't hide the pseudo-funk the familiar phrase placed him in. He gazed more or less through her as he pondered a rebuttal to her insight.

"Nevertheless," Alex spoke. Her words broke Jason's thought pattern. "I'm confident I have what you need," Alex said.

Jason was relieved to be talking business. His eyes followed hers to the display screen in front of him.

"That will get you well on your way," Alex spoke. She was referring to an enhanced enlargement of a license plate.

"Tell me," Jason said more enthused than he had been in recent moments. "This is the plate of the vehicle that our suspect got into."

"I'm very confident it is. VDOT's camera was closer and had a more powerful lens, so when I cross reference the time the suspect got into the car from the bank's tape against VDOT's camera pointed toward Jazzpers' parking lot, I get this image."

Alex manipulated the screen to display two still images, one from the bank's tape and the other from VDOT's DVD. She enlarged the image on the left, then superimposed one image on top of the other and they fit almost perfectly. When she separated the images, it was clear to Jason that the vehicle in question was a Mercedes of some sort.

"Shortly afterward, we have this," Alex continued. The bank's fuzzy image of a car was removed and replaced with an image of a Mercedes sitting at the red-light leaving Jazzpers. "We have to assume it's the same car because I've looked closely at every vehicle that entered and exited the parking lot that night. Only one Mercedes visited Jazzpers the night of Frank's death."

"Are you sure about this?"

"Look," Alex said, as she handed Jason printed pictures of the car near the lamppost and at the red light. "I'd stake my reputation on the fact that it is the same vehicle."

"That's good enough for me. I've surely gone on less. Can you show me faces?"

"Thought you'd ask. I tried. Look," Alex said as she focused and enhanced the image of the car at the light. "I'd guess that the driver is a woman," Alex continued.

"That's my thought too. You've been a great help. I have a feeling this case is about to break wide open."

"I'm sure if you have anything to do with it, it will. Your reputation precedes you."

Jason only smiled as Alex gave him a folder that contained printed images from both media to include a clear enlargement of the Mercedes license plate. He again thanked Alex before he returned to Frank's office. Even though his mental state continued to be diluted by the burden of Monique's and Frank's deaths, he walked back toward the office with more pep in his step.

Jason sat at Captain North's desk with a new energy, a newly found purpose. He expected the trace on the license plate to be back in a few short minutes and exhaled in anticipation as he began tapping a pen on the desk to combat thoughts of Monique surfacing to the forefront. For no apparent reason he began rummaging through the Captain's desk drawers. The middle drawer contained stick pins, paperclips, pens and other office supplies, but what caught Jason's ears was the rolling sound of an object. A lone golf ball made its way to the front of the drawer and bounced against the pen tray. Jason noted the brand name on the golf ball, and then brought his attention to the two golf tees sitting oddly inside of the pen tray. Jason picked up the two golf tees, closed the desk drawer and began a stick fight to pass the time. Suddenly, it saddened him when he realized that he'd never get to play the challenging game of golf with his Captain. The fantasy swordplay between the two golf tees had no meaning. The jolt of reality brought his troubles to the forefront of his mind.

Without a conscious knowledge of his actions, Jason unknowingly placed the golf tees inside his shirt pocket and attempted to place his feet on the desk. In the process he knocked to the floor Frank's cradle cell phone charger. Jason picked up the Nokia cradle, placed it back into its original position, then again began rummaging through Frank's desk drawers.

Jason found the cellphone's packaging box, read the many detailed features of the cellular device. *Verizon*, he thought. Not that Frank's cell phone provider was important, it was important to him that he and Frank had the same taste. More importantly though, were three large letters on both front and back of the box. It was a long shot, but one that Jason deemed necessary to investigate. One unique capability of the modern cell phone was its Global Positioning Satellite feature. Jason hoped that this rarely used feature was activated on Frank's cellphone. Jason was fortunate enough to speak with the same representative that Kevin spoke with when he investigated the calls to and from Frank's cell phone days before Frank's death. Jason read through Kevin's report that revealed only four calls were made to or from Frank's cell phone in the past month. He believed this to be odd because Frank was seldom seen without both his work and personal cell phones. However, Jason's direct question to the Verizon representative revealed that the GPS location feature was not inquired about previously. The Verizon representative confirmed Kevin's report about Frank's last incoming and outgoing calls and found a great joy in advising Jason that the GPS feature on Frank's cell phone was active. The Verizon representative advised Jason that it would take a while to determine the general location of Frank's cell phone if the signal could be traced.

Jason gave the Verizon representative his contact information and anxiously waited for the return call.

In the meantime, Jason performed math on the second part of the information read off of the cellphone's packaging. This information would either prove to be useful or make his anxiety for the return call from Verizon a moot point. He divided the number three hundred-sixty by twenty four. Three hundred-sixty was the maximum amount of hours that Frank's cellphone's deluxe battery could last on standby without a recharge. Fifteen days was the answer.

Two full weeks and one day, Jason thought.

"It has been twelve days since Frank's murder," Jason spoke aloud as he left Frank's office to get a desired cup of coffee.

When Jason returned from the canteen, printed information relating to the license plates was sitting on Frank's desk. He discovered that the suspected vehicle involved in Frank's death belonged to a Veronica Afferty. Her address was located in a well-to-do area in the lower eastside of Virginia City. Jason believed he was close to arresting Frank's murderer. The uncertain thing was how he would go about accomplishing the task. Characteristic of Jason was the question of protocol or not. Strangely enough, Alfredo's earlier conversation ran through his mind faster than Michael Johnson's four-hundred-meter world record time.

What would Jason do? he asked himself.

"Fuck it," Jason blurted aloud despite himself. "I'll handle this my way."

Jason could almost hear Captain North's reprimand of his decision before he'd taken any action. However, the thing that made Jason Jason, was that once he made a command decision, all regret of his actions vanished. Jason's irrational decision was based on his character in conjunction with the information received from Verizon's return call. It was like doubling down on a soft eighteen while playing Blackjack. As it turned out, the GPS signal on Frank's cell phone was active and it was determined that the cellular tower receiving Frank's signal hadn't changed in over ten days. Jason's gamble on the soft eighteen paid off. When he was told that the signal could be tracked to a two-block plus or minus radius from where it deemed to be, he believed his card on that soft eighteen was a three.

Jason gathered all information, placed it in a folder and went to the briefing room where there was on oversized replica of Virginia City's map. He placed a tack-pin at the cross streets that Verizon had given him. He drew a straight line North, South, East and West for two blocks. Jason's grid covered an area of sixteen square blocks which by more than a sheer coincidence was located in the lower east side. *Veronica Afferty*, Jason thought.

TWENTY EIGHT

Poncho Rizon was breathing heavily next to Veronica Afferty. His body was still clammy from the hip pumping that he had just performed, all five minutes' worth.

"I can't get enough of you," Poncho said still slightly winded.

"You should find yourself another lover," Veronica replied rather disgusted with his comment.

"Yeah right, you know that I only trust you."

"Then you should also trust the men I sleep with."

"What do you mean?"

"I..."

"Sshh," Poncho interrupted. "Was that a knock on your door?"

"I think so."

"You expecting someone?"

"Nope."

Veronica got out of bed, put a silky robe on her naked frame and headed for the door. She opened the door and stared blankly at Michael Jenkins.

"Toni. Toni Small?" Michael asked.

"I'm sorry, there isn't a Toni living at this address."

Michael looked at the index card in his hand, "My apologies," he said. "I must have written the address down incorrectly. Sorry to bother you, Ma'am."

"No bother at all."

Michael nodded, turned and walked away. Veronica frantically ran upstairs.

"Who was that?" Poncho asked.

"It has to be trouble," Veronica said with a worried expression carved on her face. "He asked for Toni."

"What?" Poncho bellowed excitedly.

"No shit what."

"How did he find you here?"

"Hell if I know. This isn't where you knocked his ass out."

"I thought something was fishy. I watched from the window, saw no car and saw him walk down the sidewalk."

"What are we going to do?" Veronica asked overly concerned.

"I have to go after his ass."

"Our shit is falling apart."

"Not just yet."

Michael turned the corner, crossed the street and got into Jason's car.

"Things turn out okay?" Jason asked. "You didn't feel threatened in any way, did you?"

"Not at all. I told you I'd help you. Please don't feel like you pressured me into anything."

"Very well...so, was she the same woman you encountered when your car heist occurred?"

"It's definitely her. She didn't own up to being called Toni. The hair color and style was different. She had to be wearing a wig when we met."

"How did she respond when she saw you?"

"She was very cool and collected with her act because she didn't look surprised at all. I could never mistake or forget the three small flesh moles under her right eye."

"Thank you so much. You've been a great help. I'll be in touch with you later because you'll have to come down to the station and identify her officially."

"Anytime. The bitch stole my car. Just let me know when."

"Will do. I'll be in touch," Jason said.

Michael shook Jason's hand, exited the car and got into a rental car parked directly behind Jason.

Jason drove the short distance to the front of Veronica's home. This time when she answered the door she was dressed in jeans and a tight-fitting top.

"May I help you?" she asked Jason.

"I'm Detective Jason Jerrard, Sixteenth Precinct," Jason stated while flashing his badge. "Are you Veronica Afferty?"

"I am," she responded.

Veronica reluctantly invited Jason into her home because she believed it was the best way to avoid suspicion. They stood in the foyer. The living room was to the right and a staircase that led to the second level was off-center to the left. She escorted Jason down the hall to the kitchen.

"Would you like something to drink?" Veronica asked.

"No thank you."

"Would you mind if I had tea?" she asked while opening the refrigerator.

Jason motioned for her to continue. He watched her mannerisms as she poured the beverage into the glass.

"I am so thirsty," she stated after nearly finishing the entire glass without stopping for air. "So, Detective Jared, how may I help you? Am I in some sort of trouble?"

Jason ignored the mispronunciation of his last name and proceeded to start his investigation.

"To be honest, Ma'am, you fit the description of a robbery suspect."

"What!" Veronica responded very animated. "You're kidding...this is some sick joke, right?"

"No. Actually, I have an eyewitness who claims his vehicle was stolen while being with you at another location."

"Detective Jared, doesn't that sound a little stretched?" she asked while actually separating her hands as if she were pulling on a rubber band. "This is my only home and who is this person that's attempting to incriminate me?"

Veronica poured herself a second glass of tea and Jason's observant eyes caught the slight nervousness as she conducted the act.

"He will be meeting us at the police station," Jason responded. Veronica's eyes widened, her poker face started to fade. "Do you have any aliases or go by any other names?" Jason probed.

"Veronica Afferty is my birth name. Do you consider answering to being called 'sweetheart' and 'honey' as having aliases?"

I would do exactly that, Jason thought. *Throw a bit of humor in to combat my own nervousness.* Jason smiled.

"Pet names can't be considered," Jason spoke.

"Then," Veronica replied, "Veronica Afferty is the only name that I use."

"Nevertheless, I'll need you to come to the police station to participate in a police line-up," Jason responded with his act in the game they played.

His comment was like throwing a baited hook into a body of water. The reel on the rod spun fast, the bait was swallowed. It translated into Veronica's sweat glands becoming more active than in her sex session with Poncho.

"I'd imagine you'd have better composure around cops if everything with you was on the up and up," Jason continued.

He reached behind his back, placed a set of handcuffs on the table and Veronica's tears fell heavily.

"What's going to happen to me?" Veronica asked nervously, seemingly admitting her own guilt.

"Well," Jason responded. He picked up the handcuffs and started in her direction. "It depends on your involvement with the robbery," Jason paused. "...and murder," Jason continued. He lowered more bait slowly into the water.

Veronica's eyes widened even more. She gave Jason a dead-man's stare before the deep heavy sigh that coincided with her eyes being shut. Jason took her mannerisms as the second bait being swallowed.

"May I at least put on a pair of shoes?" Veronica asked as her eyes slowly opened.

"Yes, but understand that I must follow you to where your shoes are."

Veronica didn't speak; she tilted her head indicating to Jason to follow her.

"Did you recognize the man at your door moments ago?" Jason asked as they ascended the stairs.

"What's the point of lying now?" Veronica responded. She reached the top of the stairs, turned around to Jason who was two steps from the top.

"That man at my door before you was just one of many that we conned," she confessed.

Veronica's head shook at Jason's urgency to pump her for information before they even reached the police station.

"Can you explain who the 'we' is?" Jason pushed.

"We as in people that I work with?" Veronica said evasively.

"And, where would I find these people?" Jason asked somewhat sarcastically.

"They are around," she answered in a flat tone.

"Would one of these people walk with a limp?" Jason asked as if he were inquiring "how was your day?"

Jason realized he'd struck a nerve when Veronica acknowledged his question with a troubled facial expression without a spoken word. When she lowered herself to a knee at the side of the bed in search of her shoes, Jason instinctively released the strap that secured his pistol in the holster. His hand lowered to the side when he noticed the pair of denim shoes in Veronica's hand.

Okay then, Jason thought.

He studied her carefully while she put on the shoes. Something wasn't right. All of Jason's senses knew it. He felt an eeriness like the thick dampness of a heavy humidity day.

"Are you alone?" Jason asked.

"Why? Looking at my ass got to you?" Veronica asked for no other reason other than to irritate him. Jason's expression told her that he wasn't amused. "You and I are the only ones here."

"Then, you'd not object to me looking around a bit?" Jason asked.

"Sure, look all you want, just as soon as I see a search warrant. I'll go to the police station, but you looking for a ghost when no spirits are here is a fruitless effort."

Veronica's sudden defensive posture demanded Jason on all fours. He bent his elbows and glanced under the bed. Admittedly he was surprised that no one was hiding under it. Still his senses warned him of imminent danger.

Dumb move on my part, Jason thought as he began to stand.

Rapid heavy footsteps grew louder and stronger toward him. *Back*, Jason's impulse told him. Without thinking or understanding the cause for his alarm, Jason flipped and fell to his back. The maneuver was less than a second faster than the bat that Poncho swung at his head. Jason felt the breeze, heard the swish sound that the high velocity swing made.

"Poncho! No!" Veronica screamed.

Poncho ignored his sister's plea of non-violence. He cocked the bat back again to strike his make-shift baseball. Jason was scrambling backward for his life and rolled sideways to prevent bodily harm. He felt as though his head had replaced the amusement parks' gopher's head that usually popped out of a hole to be swatted down with an oversized mallet. The constant ducking, dodging and rolling from the deadly bat prevented Jason from drawing his pistol. One instance, Jason sat on the floor legs spread, Poncho had the bat high over his head and thrust the bat straight down reminiscent of splitting firewood. Jason swiftly crab-walked backward on his hands and feet, only to have his back splat against the wall with a good amount of force.

Jason's *"Damn"* thought hadn't finished processing through his brain when the bat came thundering down between his legs, just short of destroying his manhood. The bat hit with so much force that it bounced off the carpet as if a lightning bolt had been repelled by a rubber mat. Jason's quick reflexes enabled him to grab the bat tightly with one hand before Poncho could prepare another assault. The two men struggled for dominance over the wooden object. Poncho's physique, though sloppy, proved to be a worthy opponent for Jason. Poncho handled Jason's weight easier than Frank's dead-weight body. He secured a stable stance with both hands clutched on the bat's handle and then methodically took half-steps backward reminiscent of a plane pull.

Jason's one-handed grip was equally secure on the bat. With each step taken by Poncho, Jason was pulled from the sitting position to a standing one. Jason's reach for his pistol coincided with Poncho's raised leg to kick him in the chest.

"Whoa there, fella," Jason warned. "It's time to end this baseball game. Drop the bat; get on your fucking knees with your hands behind your back, fingers locked."

Jason released the bat and steadied his aim with both hands. Poncho's last act of defiance forced him to pull the bat back, cocked, ready for an unlikely deadly strike to Jason's head.

"Got skills?" Jason asked. "You couldn't hit my large ass; what the fuck makes you think you can bat away a speeding bullet."

"Poncho no!" Veronica yelled. "Please drop the bat. No more killing. No one has to die," she pleaded to Jason. "Please don't shoot him, he is my brother."

"Your brother's ass will get dropped here and now," Jason commanded, "if he doesn't do as I say," Jason said just short of yelling.

Poncho backed away from Jason, stuck in the bat-ready position. Veronica became the referee of the match; she frantically positioned herself between the two men. Her arms spread wide falsely keeping the two apart.

"Poncho, it's over," she said nervously.

"It ain't over," Poncho yelled. "I'm not jailin'."

Jason ignored Poncho's colorful term for being in jail and let his arrogance show.

"Unless you're a descendant of Houdini and can vanish in thin air, I will arrest your ass for the murder of my Captain."

Jason dropped the aim at Poncho, spread his arms wide with the pistol dangling not on the trigger, but on the trigger guard. He dared Poncho to make a move.

"Realistically," Jason boasted. "Dead or alive, I'm content with either condition that your twisted mind desires," Jason spoke in a monotone.

"Not today," Poncho countered.

Veronica screamed as she was snatched roughly and abruptly from behind by Poncho. Her vocal bellow immediately transformed into a gasp, a choke, a struggle for air. Poncho secured the bat around her neck with great force. Veronica labored in vain to remove the bat that had already begun crushing her windpipe.

"You're a lunatic if you think that crazy-ass move is going to work on me," Jason countered. "Besides, she is your sister, asshole!"

Poncho applied more pressure against Veronica's throat. He leaned back and nearly lifted her from the floor. Veronica had very little weight, if any, on the tips of her toes. Consequently, signs of strangulation developed more rapidly.

"You fuckin' prick," Poncho stated near laughter. "Veronica, Toni, Daiquiri, Kaylyn or whatever name she goes by means little to me. This whore is my sister and I've been molesting her since she was ten years old. It was me who popped her cherry, so what makes you think that I give a rat's ass if the bitch dies by my hands. Do you think you can shoot me before I snap the bitch's neck?"

By this time, Poncho had Veronica suspended in the air by the bat. Her struggle ceased, arms fell to her sides and her body twitched as if she received electrical impulses.

"Okay, okay!" Jason responded in an act of desperation.

Jason carefully placed the pistol's hammer back in the fired position, engaged the safety button, kneeled and placed the weapon on the floor.

"Kick that shit away," Poncho instructed.

Jason's leg moved sideways and the pistol slid quietly on the carpet and settled under a wingback chair.

"Now," Jason said calmly, "let her go. There is no need for her to die."

"That's right, fucker, you'll never get the upper hand on me because I don't give a shit about anyone but me. Understand now."

Poncho released the fat part of the bat, but continued to hold the handle with the other hand at his side. Veronica's body fell hard to the carpet seemingly lifeless. Jason studied her for a quick moment; he couldn't ascertain if she was breathing or not. Suddenly, she choked, gasped for air. That deemed to be the starting bell for Jason and Poncho's next round of their bout. An array of bat swings began, intended to inflict serious bodily harm on Jason. Jason ducked and dodged the assault successfully for all but one attack. A forceful blow connected with Jason's upper right arm, the impact knocked him backward into the wingback chair. He and the chair tumbled to the floor.

Poncho jumped into the air over the downed chair like a ninja with the deadly blow of the bat held high above his head. Poncho had started the kill strike's descent in midair when suddenly Jason sprang to his feet. Timed perfectly, Jason struck Poncho in the chest with his fist before Poncho's blow had passed his eye level. Poncho was forced backward; he splattered onto the floor on his back. He sought to replenish the air jolted from him upon connecting with the floor. He lost the bat during the fall.

"What the fuck?" Poncho said as the extreme pain running through his chest announced itself.

Poncho felt wetness run down his body and begin to soak through his shirt. He moved his hand to the pained area and found two items protruding out of his chest just above the top right ribs.

"What the hell did you do to me?" Poncho asked upon looking down at his chest.

"What? No more Hank Aaron homerun swings?" Jason responded sarcastically.

While Jason was concealed behind the wingback chair, he reached into his shirt pocket, placed two golf tees respectively between the left and right side of his middle finger, clutched a tight fist and had a deadly two-pronged weapon.

Poncho sat up and looked at Jason in disbelief.

"You stabbed me with two fucking golf tees," Poncho stated wryly.

"All is fair in love and war," Jason commented. "You're the one who introduced sports in a man fight. The way I see it, I was your baseball and you became the ground for the golf tees."

"Injured or not, I'm still not jailin'," Poncho responded with defiance.

Two loud gunfire blasts startled Jason. He dove to the floor after the bat.

"He's not going to jail. I sent him to hell!" Veronica said with cold trembled emotions.

Veronica had gained enough strength to retrieve Jason's pistol during the man-fight between Jason and Poncho. One of Veronica's deadly bullets went through Poncho's throat; the other was directly between the eyes. Splattered brains from the explosive round exited the back of Poncho's head like a fire hydrant's cap blown off from intense pressure.

Jason's heart raced. Defenseless, he expected that he'd be the next target. Veronica aimed the pistol centered at Jason's chest and slowly walked toward him. She tossed the pistol to the carpet, steered her eyes toward her slain brother and sobbed heavily.

TWENTY NINE

Veronica's tears continued to fall while she knelt over her brother's body.

"I told him very recently," Veronica said rather calmly considering the fury of mixed emotions running through her, "that I'd kill him if he ever placed his hands on me again. It's all over now."

Jason wasn't certain of the meaning of the last sentence until Veronica continued her story with details of a sick twisted family history.

"He started molesting me when I was ten," Veronica announced distraughtly. "He is," Veronica's eyes moved from the dead body to Jason, "he was eleven years older than me. My dysfunctional life started with him peeking at me when I showered. In retrospect, me being naïve, young and willing to accept the hush money that he gave me to keep quiet was the beginning of his end.

"The whole sick thing turned into him sneaking into my bedroom late at night. First, all he would do was finger me and I vowed that I'd tell my parents. But I ultimately believed him when he told me that I'd be put on an adoption list and put in a home with people that cared nothing for me if I'd ever told anyone about what he was doing.

"I knew what my clit was at age twelve. He started sleeping with me before my fifteenth birthday." Veronica paused, held her eyes shut tightly in silence for a long moment. Her body shook as she recalled painful memories from the past. "I was being sold to his friends at age sixteen. He would always be the last one to get some. To this day, I'm disillusioned as to why, what, or how he completely gained my cooperation, silence and control over me. The whole thing just manifested from my early age to today. I do know that as I grew older, I enjoyed what money I received. Eventually, he talked me into the scheme of robbing men of their cars."

Veronica confessed her soul as if Jason were a priest. He assumed that her emotional baggage had to be unpacked and thrown away. Jason empathized for her.

"For the most part," she continued after another moment of silence, "I'd grown accustomed to sleeping with him, but the day of your Captain's murder should have been the first and last time I was hit by him. Sleeping with him, yes, but hitting me was a line that I couldn't tolerate and should have never been crossed."

Jason kept a straight face considering the notion that her warped thoughts made little sense to him.

"Have there been more murders?" Jason asked.

"As far as I know, the murder thing was something new and was most likely committed because Frank was a cop. Odd things started happening before that though. Poncho suddenly developed a need to mark our conquests as if they were cattle. He attached the pin stolen from your Captain to the top of his cane that he sometimes used because of his limp, heated it and branded the Michael character and others as a reminder of their stupidity."

All that glitters isn't gold, she thought.

"I have a sense," Jason spoke sympathetically, "of what you've endured throughout the years. Understand what I must now do."

Veronica's eyes left the slain prey to the dangling pair of handcuffs on Jason's pointer-finger. The handcuffs propelled thoughts to the forefront that she was in fact a murderer; tears multiplied, seemingly descending from a troubled waterfall. She stood, placed her hands behind her back without uttering a word. Jason placed the handcuffs on her wrists with the hands in front of her body instead. Jason sat the wingback chair upright, intended for Veronica's use; instead she sat next to her brother and viewed him with a look that Jason couldn't determine.

Jason picked up and placed in his shirt pocket a shiny object found on the carpet upon resetting the wingback chair upright. He patted around his belt in search for his cellphone, and then realized that the device was left in his car.

"Phone?" Jason asked.

Jason followed her eyes to the location of the cordless, retrieved the handset and sat in the wingback chair. He made two calls. One was to the Sixteenth Precinct to report the murder and arrest of suspects involved in Frank's murder. The second call was more for his personal gratification. Seconds after the ten digits were dialed, Frank's cell phone vibrated in his shirt pocket. When the voicemail greeting invaded his ears, Jason ended the call, satisfied with himself as a detective, yet saddened once again by the loss of his friend. As Jason waited for the cavalry of police officers to arrive, he asked Veronica the one question that plagued him the most.

"You guys cleaned up and disappeared without a trace after taking Michael's car; why would you not leave here knowing that a police officer had been murdered?"

"Poncho didn't think that it was necessary," Veronica responded. "Dead men tell no tales, he told me."

"Their ghosts sometimes do," Jason added.

Sirens from the arriving onslaught of police cars intercepted their ears.

THIRTY

Back at the station, Kevin was relieved that Jason had brought Frank's murderers to justice so quickly. However, he sounded much like the slain superior when he reprimanded Jason for his lack of proper protocol.

"Kevin," Jason stated, interrupting the unwanted lecture, "you know how I do things so save it for someone who gives a shit."

Kevin frowned; startled that Jason would have an attitude with him.

Monique's death must be eating him up inside, Kevin thought as means to rationalize Jason's posture.

Yet, Jason's tone bothered him even though he tried to hide it. Emotionally distraught or not, Kevin believed he deserved more respect than that. Therefore, he gave Jason an "off the record" piece of mind. Jason politely took the verbal bashing for no other reason than to let Kevin vent. After a very short while, Jason turned, walked away with one hand in the air; it signified that he had heard enough. He closed Frank's office door rudely in Kevin's face. Jason sat at the desk, anticipating an angrier verbal lashing from Kevin, but, Kevin was too shocked by Jason's actions to follow him inside the office space.

Kevin turned away and thought, *Man, that guy has serious issues right now*.

Jason crossed his arms on the desk in front of him, laid his head on the self-made pillow and began questioning himself. His short fuse with Kevin, Monique's death, Frank's death and other negative thoughts plagued him as he somehow was able to begin detailing the facts of Poncho's death in a police report. This time writing the report was painfully agonizing. It took far longer than expected.

Jason finished the report, walked to Kevin's desk and handed him the report. Kevin studied him, unsure of how to read Jason's expression.

"All of the details are here," Jason said as they made the exchange. "Everything prior and up to my call to the station is contained within. If you have additional questions, you can reach me by cellphone."

Kevin nodded. It was a motion that Jason didn't see because he turned, then walked away without another word.

Jason found himself entering Rosalina's near closing time. He briefly spoke to Delia en route to his booth. Delia became alarmed, but not only with Jason's impersonal attitude. Something within alerted her that he had been through a war based on the few minor bruises Jason had sustained from his acrobatic tumbling on Veronica's floor.

Delia went to her loved one, Alfredo. Thus, Alfredo was the deliverer of Jason's food.

"How are things with you?" Alfredo asked while he placed Jason's food on the table.

"My dear friend," Jason responded. "You wouldn't believe me if I told you."

"It may be worth a try," Alfredo countered.

"Sometime later," Jason suggested as he poured himself a cup of coffee.

"Very well," Alfredo said. He knew his friend, understood that in time Jason would open up to him. However, Alfredo's next words of caution came directly from his heart. "Do yourself a favor and don't shut down again. I'm here whenever you need me."

The two men stared at each other for a moment, caringly in silence. Alfredo believed he'd translated the message correctly for Jason. He released his gaze, left his dear friend to combat the troublesome emotions in his own manner. Jason pushed his food to the side, exited Rosalina's without Alfredo's or Delia's knowledge.

THIRTY ONE

North and South were two men who were not as muscular and physically demanding as Dakota. Together, they were a force to be reckoned with. Kal Lincoln was North. He was a few years younger than Dakota and was the scout for potential clients for the notorious group named "The Combined States." South was Devon Williams, the most athletic of the three. Together, North, South and Dakota were the muscle behind collecting monies due to their hired clients. Dakota's moonlighting with Sly on the side was the only time the three weren't together.

Even with Dakota's imprisonment, the threesome had a sense of their ultimate power. A false feeling because things were entirely different. Dakota was wheelchair stricken. He would no longer be the massive beast and terror he once was. Doctors had told Dakota that once his knee mended from Jason's destruction, he'd surely walk with a limp and his mobility would be limited. Jason's arrest of him and Delia's testimony had put him behind bars for the rest of his life. Dakota's saving grace from a death sentence was the fact that the Mayor's wife hadn't died. Dakota had summoned North and South for the first time since his incarceration.

Dakota was in a large room with several other inmates. Armed guards, three with shotguns, stood near each wall of the rectangular room. The room had four rows of tables and chair sets, four deep. Less than half of the available sixteen tables were occupied on this visitor's day. Therefore, the inmates sat separated, sparingly throughout the room.

"How are you handling this place?" South asked Dakota.

"I've been better," Dakota responded emotionless.

"And the knee," North chimed in.

Dakota rubbed a hand on the cast supporting the damaged knee as if the friction's warmth somehow helped repair the mangled knee.

"I'll recover," Dakota stated sadly. "I'll need to use a cane for the rest of my life. Me!" Dakota stated very animated with a disgust that burned him like acid on his skin. "Enough about me," Dakota said, attempting to keep his pressure down. "How are you two?"

Dakota nodded in a manner that gave South permission to speak first.

"We're fine," South immediately responded. "Admittedly, the gang isn't the same without you."

"You'll adapt. Continue business as usual. If any of my knowledge can be useful to you, then I'm at your disposal."

"Act three is about to begin," South said cheerfully.

"Good, good. Having said that, here are instructions on how to access the monies to keep the operation running. Half of it, however, will be used to buy my protection because I'm not tossing no fucking body's salad."

North and South giggled internally, Dakota's statement struck a funny bone with both, but out of respect for their longtime friend, they simply nodded sincerely.

"I guess it will be hard maintaining your toughness with your knee in its current condition," North stated.

"Maybe. But, understand that I'll bite a muther-fucker's dick off before I freely do something like that."

This time those words relayed by Dakota's baritone voice ignited an outward hysterical laugh from North and South.

"What I said might sound stupid," Dakota continued, "but believe me, I'll use my teeth on a fucker's dick like a Ginsu knife."

North and South appreciated Dakota's effort in making light of his situation. They'd known Dakota for years, knew that he didn't like school because of recess and knew that Dakota's shown toughness was for their benefit. They were saddened; this would be the last time the three of them would be seen together. Dakota handed South a folded piece of legal paper from his shirt pocket.

"Here are the instructions on how to obtain the money I promised you," Dakota said.

With that, Dakota abruptly wheeled himself backward, quickly turned around and rolled the wheelchair away as fast as his massive arms would allow. He left the two without saying a word, without the slightest good-bye, without showing them how painful his predicament truly was for him. Both North and South rose from their chairs, seemingly signifying that a military General was leaving the building. They sensed Dakota's anguish, understood the beast in captivity syndrome. When Dakota turned the corner out of sight, they glanced at each other, nodded and turned to walk away.

THIRTY TWO

North and South watched Jason exit Rosalina's. Dakota's instructions in the encrypted letter simply stated that he wanted Jason to be gone. It was at their discretion to handle the situation any way they saw fit. They had formulated ACT III's action plan to be painful, personal inflicted physical pain and their starring roles started as Jason descended Rosalina's steps. South drove away in a separate vehicle while North waited behind as Jason headed toward his car. Jason's usual alertness was dampened by thoughts of Monique's death that invaded him like a swarm of bees on honey. He barely remembered the drive out of the city to the more rural suburbs. As usual for Jason, this particular two-lane road felt as though it was solely his. The fewer streetlights gave Jason a better view of the stars and the fewer traffic lights made his ride home more pleasant. All except for one traffic light that he never seemed to catch on green.

"I got you this time," Jason announced aloud as he pushed harder on the accelerator. "It's about...damn!" left his mouth.

Not again, it's a fucking conspiracy! Jason thought as his foot pivoted to the brake from the accelerator. Tonight was no different from other nights. He sat with the red glow from the traffic light taunting him as if it were possessed. Jason closed his eyes and sighed in disbelief.

"Damn it," Jason stated in a more excited manner.

His eyes opened quickly, correlating to the sudden rush of his heartbeat caused by an unexpected movement with his car. Jason was hit from behind by another vehicle. Jason looked into the rearview mirror and saw the driver of the car behind him exit his vehicle to assess the damage.

Jason unfastened his seatbelt and joined the man investigating the potential damage. The man attempted to scrape his car's paint from Jason's bumper with a small pocketknife. Jason gave him an inquisitive look.

"I'm just trying to see if the paint could be easily removed without the aid of a body shop," North stated before putting the knife back into his pocket. "Are you alright, Sir?"

"Yes, I believe so. You have faulty brakes or something?"

"No, my foot slipped off the brake and when my car moved forward, I tried too quickly to stop it and slammed the accelerator down instead of my brake. Good thing I wasn't too far away from your car, otherwise the damage could have been more severe."

First glance at his vehicle, Jason saw only very minor paint damage. He noted that the other vehicle's front bumper had crumpled and hadn't pushed the flexible plastic cover back to the original shape. Jason fought the notion of getting upset with it being one of his new cars, a car that he had never driven. Nor did he give a second thought to his pride in keeping his vehicles well conditioned. His BMW was over four years old, but both the interior and exterior still had a showroom luster. The black scrape from the opposing car's bumper meant little, as did his car and all of his worldly possessions because he'd gladly give it all up to have Monique back, waiting for him to return home.

"May I see your license and registration?" Jason asked because there might have been hidden damages that the stars and traffic light's glow couldn't reveal.

"Sure," North complied. He reached into his wallet and pulled a pen from his shirt pocket.

Uneasiness swept Jason. He wasn't certain why until he felt himself falling to the pavement street. South had hit Jason in the back of the knees with a thick metal pipe. North and South were true to their form. North began attacking Jason above the waist while South continued his assault below Jason's waist.

Jason was taken by complete surprise. His ill feeling about the attack was far too late for him to mount any defensive measures. In a quick lapse of time, the duo had beaten Jason to the ground barely conscious. Jason's body was bombarded with a barrage of kicking and stomping until it was believed that he was on the brink of death. North and South lifted Jason's tattered body and placed him in the passenger's seat of his vehicle. Jason's body fell against the window, reminiscent of someone sleeping, but he was far beyond that. Only the heavens knew why he continued to breathe. Several fresh bruises and lacerations decorated his face, but they compared little to the several broken ribs and bruised sternum. Even though Jason's breathing was silent, his breaths were short and jerky with each expansion of the chest.

South's vehicle was abandoned and set on fire in a nearby cornfield. South drove closely behind North in North's car. North drove toward Three Pond Park with reckless abandonment and excessive speed despite the warnings given to him from South via cellphone. North's primary drive was to dispose of Jason's body and then collect more monies from Dakota. However, the last traffic light prior to entering the park had other plans. He was too far away to accelerate through to catch the light yellow. Therefore, he braked heavily and the rapid deceleration forced Jason's limp body from the window toward the dashboard. Jason's head bounded off of the area just above the glove compartment and settled between his legs. His arms flung haphazardly forward, connected with the dash and hung toward the floor. Jason's body position resembled one of an airline passenger preparing for crash landing, absent the arms clutched around the knees.

South cut the lift gates lock that secured entry into Three Pond Park with heavy-duty cutters, raised the metal bar so they could enter and lowered the bar afterward to make it appear unaltered. North headed for the third pond, the largest of the three manmade bodies of water enclosed within the boundaries of Three Pond Park. This one housed the ramp that allowed jet skis to be placed into the water. Their plan was to drown Jason.

Jason lifted his woozy head and turned it toward North. A surprised North began furiously pounding Jason in the head with his fist. Jason resisted North's assault for as long as he could, but ultimately his battered body conceded to North's will. He collapsed back into an identical uncon-scious position as North reached the boat ramp that descended into the water. North used the whitewashed medium- to large-sized boulders that aligned both sides of the boat ramp to center the vehicle at the top of the ramp. He unfastened the seatbelt just as Jason moved again. This time North abused Jason with both hands. Jason's left arm rose for protection. South noticed North's confrontation and dashed to his partner's aid. South stopped in his tracks when he heard two gunshots from Jason's backup revolver that was concealed and not discovered by his attackers.

Suddenly, the engine roared, the vehicle surged forward with spinning tires. With a short distance to travel down the ramp, but with the accel-erator fully depressed, the vehicle plunged into the water, floated a good distance away and slowly began to sink. South watched helplessly awed.

The Crossfire's convertible seals leaked water as if they were non-existent. Quickly the vehicle began to fill with dark and gloomy water. The extremely cold water overloaded Jason's survival instincts. As the car sank, the water level rose from his waist to the chest. Jason tilted his head backward as the frigid water overtook his neck. He took a huge deep breath of air, then submerged himself into the cold murky water. He blindly felt inside of the car's interior until he found the door button.

It's locked, his mind echoed when he depressed the button to open the door.

The thing Jason admired most about the vehicle was that without a key or the vehicle being on, the doors couldn't be opened. Therefore, the electronic key-fob transmitter inside the car was useless. Nevertheless, he pressed all buttons on the device several times in succession, but the door remained locked. All of the vehicle's electrical circuitry shorted right after the engine stalled during the descent to the bottom of the pond.

What a great theft deterrent, Jason oddly thought despite his predicament.

The further the car dove into nothingness, the colder the water became for Jason. His fingers were cold and they cramped while making a fist. He positioned his body to somehow kick out the back window as North's body floated into him and hindered the process. Jason's quick thinking allowed him to remember the pocketknife that North used on the bumper. Jason retrieved the three-inch blade from North's pants and for the first time opened his eyes in the murky water. Blackness was all that he saw. Therefore, he used the remainder of his tangled senses, floated to the rear and carved out an escape route around the outside of the rear glass window.

Time was crucial, his air was out; nothing but an extreme will to live could keep him from drowning. He pushed the glass away and frantically swam to the surface. Panicked by uncertainty, his eyes opened to ascertain just how far he had to go before he could capture the much needed air.

That's the moon, he thought. The faint round object's glow barely penetrated its luminescence beyond the water's surface, but the thought itself became the incentive that kept his mouth closed even though his lungs ached to inhale. Continued life was a few feet away. He felt the whisper of a cool breeze through his hair, then across his face as he rose from the depths of the water. However, Jason hastily treated himself to fresh air much too soon. His reward was air substituted by a mouthful of water that choked him as most of it was drained down the breathing pipe. He managed to tread water through the sudden breathing frenzy, regain his breath and stockpile enough strength in the process to start the swim to safety.

The moon provided ample light that helped Jason determine the location of the boat ramp. Jason's thirty-foot swim seemed like two-hundred yards because of his battered body. When his swim stroke hand touched the cement boat ramp, Jason came to his knees, rested for a brief moment and negotiated the upslope on his hands and knees. Jason moved slowly until the only part of his body that remained in the water was his feet. He collapsed, breathed heavily, his wet freezing body lay on the cold cement. He felt an extreme pain that the cold water induced on him and now that that particular form of death was behind him, the discomfort of North and South's beating inundated him. Jason's initial thought was warmth and his need for it. He repeated the mental desire for warmth as if it would combat the elements and warm his frigid body.

Jason's *"There were two of them"* thought had no effect on warming him, yet the reflective thought caused further anxiety, alerted his survival instincts.

He pushed the pain away; in one continuous movement, Jason flipped to his back, pulled the backup revolver from his waist and pointed it overhead at South who tried to sneak up on him. The threatening sight of Jason's pistol stopped South dead in his tracks as South held a large-sized white-washed boulder, apparently a heavy one because he struggled holding the solid object's weight over his head. His arms trembled. South fancied Jason as a kid's plastic green army rifleman lying in the prone position, except Jason was on his back with his head tilted backward to view South.

Jason had a deadly aim at South. He knew it.

"Fuck it," Jason announced and pulled the trigger with intent to kill.

The gun simply clicked, Jason's eyes widened from despair. The simple sound gave South an adrenaline rush that strengthened his arms. He balanced the boulder straight armed over his head and smiled now that he had the upper hand over Jason.

"You're lucky to have survived the pond, but your ass won't survive this big fucking rock. Dakota," South grunted as he moved the boulder forward to smash Jason's pumpkin-like head, "will thoroughly enjoy how I describe your death."

Defeated, Jason's arms became heavier. The gun suddenly felt like it weighed a ton. Jason closed his eyes and hoped that his death would be quick.

"I bet your ass never thought you'd become a husband and a widower all in the span of five minutes, did you?"

"You killed Monique!" Jason yelled. "You bastard!"

"Yes. It was very sweet, wasn't it? One deadly bullet at the height of your joy."

Jason yelled as if a chainsaw were cutting into his chest. He heard the flesh tear, the sound of bones and cartilage being ripped and torn into shreds by the revolving steel chain. His own heartbeat echoed like a past dream in his ears.

"Aargh," Jason bellowed while he pulled the trigger several times rapidly.

The desperate attempt filled Jason's ears with the sound of several mis-fired chambers. Between the disappointment and despair of the non-exploded shells were two pop sounds that had a familiar ring to them. Two bullets entered South's chest, exploded out of his back as if they were destined to reach the stars, and left behind a large fist-sized black hole at this back. The delayed response of South's body collapsing was almost comical. First South's knees buckled; he fell onto them with the boulder still held overhead. The rock slipped through his hands, impacted with his head and somehow performed a balancing act through the process of South's body falling to the ground.

Jason stood, looked down at his latest conquest, felt an urge to kick him, but his battered, cold body failed to muster enough energy to lift his foot. Jason glanced toward the pond, and then directed his attention back to South. The disbelief over his most recent history turned into confusion that manifested itself into anger. Jason's temperature rose, he felt blood rush to his head, and to his feet like he'd just walked on the sun.

"What the fuck did I do to you?" Jason yelled.

Then it hit him, the ton of bricks lifted from his heart. Instantly, Jason had the answer to the question that his heart yearned for. Though he was battered, bruised and on the brink of death, the "who" answer gave him a sense of peace. South's comment was meant to be a dagger to destroy his spirit and fight, but on the contrary, it provided the answer of who was behind Monique's death.

THIRTY THREE

Jason sat in South's vehicle with his forehead resting on the steering wheel. The car's heater had yet to warm his freezing body; however, that discomfort and the battered condition of his body compared little to the revengeful thoughts inundating him.

That muther-fucker, Jason thought repeatedly.

He found South's cell phone on the seat and called the Sixteenth Precinct. Jason in the meantime talked with Alfredo. Jason's "not to worry" words about the attack became wasted vibrations in Alfredo's ears. A troublesome agreement was reached between the great friends to meet at Memorial Hospital after the authorities had arrived. Their conversation was shortened further by the arrival of many police officers. In a very short time, the area was swamped with police activity. Sgt. Austin was the first to arrive. He tapped on the driver's side window and startled Jason whose bodily condition forced him to rest. Yet, Jason's senses were sharp even in the estranged condition; Jason swung the empty revolver toward the tapping sound that he heard lightning fast.

"Jas, it's me!" Sgt. Austin recited excitedly while he ducked behind the safety of the car door.

Jason stepped out of the car, detailed the turn of events to Kevin and then let the paramedics assess his condition. Jason refused the ambulance ride to Memorial Hospital, elected to drive himself there in South's car. Along the way, he requested Dr. Bodou as his attending physician.

As Jason walked into the emergency room, Alfredo jumped to his feet. In a hurried and excited pace, he placed an arm around Jason's shoulder.

"Careful," Jason said. He grimaced in pain. "I ache all over."

"My God," Alfredo responded. "What has happened to you? You were so evasive on the phone."

"Besides a dramatic beating and nearly being drowned, I'm okay...I suppose. I drove myself here. So, I'd guess my condition isn't too serious. However, I'll leave my diagnosis to Dr. Bodou's assessment."

"Do you have the strength to tell me more details about what happened to you?" Alfredo asked.

Jason was holding up fairly well considering his past hours or so. He started detailing an abbreviated version of his most recent escapade when he blacked out. He fell to the floor like a sheet dropped while being folded. Alfredo rushed to his friend's aid and had a hand behind Jason's head when consciousness returned to Jason.

"Can I get some help here?" Alfredo shouted as he looked around.

Alfredo noticed two emergency room technicians and Dr. Bodou racing toward them with a gurney in tow. The technicians helped Jason to his feet, but Jason refused the recommendation to lie on the gurney.

"I'm okay now. I can walk, it was just a dizzy spell," Jason said.

"Mr. Jerrard," Dr. Bodou spoke. "Just looking at you contradicts what you just said. At first glance, I'd say the dizziness was related to your battered condition. So, let me attend to you the best way that I see fit."

"You're the expert, but I'm not lying down on that thing," Jason stated while he looked at the gurney.

The emergency room technicians held Jason on both sides, escorted him to the examination room with a troubled Alfredo close by.

"Who did this to you?" Alfredo again asked his friend with a more persistent tone.

"I don't really know," Jason lied. "I left Rosalina's for home. When I got out of the city, someone hit my car while at a light. While checking out the damage, I was attacked."

"What!"

"Seriously, I'm capable of handling myself in a fight, but I was completely taken by surprise and beaten unconscious."

"Who would do such a thing?" Alfredo asked.

Crystin's revenge ran through Alfredo's mind. Equal to Jason's knowledge of Monique, Jason understood how Alfredo thought. He sensed Alfredo's hypothesis and corrected his close friend's thought.

"Trust me," Jason said. His half-hearted smile was followed by, "the Mayor's wife thing is over."

Uh-huh, Alfredo thought as he handed Jason the requested fresh change of clothes.

"In two sentences or less, can you tell me why your clothes are wet?"

"One sentence...I almost drowned."

"This is no time for jokes," Alfredo responded.

Jason's raised brow signified, *No kidding*.

"My guess is that they were going to run my car into the pond while I was unconscious. But I woke up, spoiled the plan. I did, however, find myself sinking to the bottom seemingly doomed."

"Life throws us curve balls from time to time. It seems that you're proficient at bat because you are alive and that's all that matters."

"Jason," Dr. Bodou interrupted. "I have an examination room available when you're ready."

"Excuse me," Jason said to Alfredo. "I won't be long." Jason looked at his physician. "I hope."

Jason sat on the examining table wearing the paper gown. As much as he hated them, it proved to be a greater comfort than his damp clothes.

"What kind of madness can a retired detective get into?" Dr. Bodou asked.

"I wish I knew the cause..." Jason paused to reflect on his sentence. "I have unknown enemies or maybe I look like the type that likes to be bullied around or, maybe some people hold grudges."

Jason knew it to be the latter. That memory would serve him later.

"What you're telling me is...you don't know why you're in this condition."

"True," Jason lied again. "I'm lost. I haven't been back in town long enough to make enemies or cause trouble. Monique and I spent more than two months vacationing in the Caribbean. I come back to my Captain's death. Then, my world was completely swept away with the devastation of Monique's murder. Now, I get jumped by two thugs. What could possibly happen next?"

"You're expecting more mayhem to happen?"

"I certainly hope not, but drama normally comes in threes."

"You don't actually believe that, do you?"

"Let's just call it an old wives tale."

"You shouldn't speak into existence anything negative," Dr. Bodou said.

Jason reflected on the serious tone his physician had and pondered the doctor's comment for a moment. Brought from the depths of his beliefs, *You can have what you say*, popped into his mind.

"You may be on to something," Jason spoke. "Somewhere in the Bible there is a verse, loosely translated, it goes like this. 'I told my people that they can have what they say, instead they are saying what they have.'"

Dr. Bodou's head titled to the side with an eyebrow raised. He was considering Jason's words.

"I see how that can relate to my comment," Dr. Bodou responded.

There was a brief awkward moment of silence between the men before the doctor performed Jason's examination. Considering the thrashing Jason had undergone, his condition wasn't too serious. Luckily, none of his ribs were completely broken, but he had sustained three severely fractured ones. He also had minor lacerations on his face and body with the exception of a cut in the middle of his forehead that required six stitches. Jason was assured by Dr. Bodou that the swelling on the back of his head wasn't a blood clot. Dr. Bodou also prescribed a pain medication along with a serious caution to take it easy for a few days.

"What about the fainting spell earlier?" Jason asked concerned.

"I wouldn't be too alarmed about that. Sometimes our body mimics a computer and has to reboot itself. Your fainting was just that."

Jason didn't respond to Dr. Bodou's explanation. He basically considered it as the doctor telling him that he had a virus when no better explanation was available. Jason's facial expression prompted the doctor's next words.

"I'll request that you undergo a few tests to determine the cause of the dizziness," Dr. Bodou said.

"Thank you."

Dr. Bodou updated Jason's records in the computer, wrote down a number for Jason to call to schedule the tests on a piece of paper.

"My recommendation for the tests are in your records now, just call this number and arrange them," Dr. Bodou said as he passed Jason the folded piece of paper and the prescription. "Take these two pills now and continue with the rest as detailed on the prescription bottle."

"Thank you again. I can use these now."

"Take care of yourself and get plenty of rest," the doctor advised before he left the room.

Jason changed into the dry clothes and sat on the bed wondering how he would soothe his friend's worry. The task at hand was to convince Alfredo that their restaurant partnership would continue for a long time.

"Something wrong?" Alfredo asked when he entered the examination room. "The doctor said it was okay to enter now."

"I'm fine," Jason responded. He stood, yet supported his weight against the examination table. "I was taking a moment to reflect on my non-provoked attack."

"Are you seriously injured?" Alfredo asked.

Alfredo's eyes peered at Jason's stitching. Jason knew Alfredo well enough to understand that his friend was abreast of his condition. Hell hadn't frozen over, so the chance of him not pumping the doctor for information was slim, very slim.

"I'll live. A little rest and Neosporin would go a long way right now."

"My friend, please don't take your condition lightly. Being in water that cold even for a short time could have an adverse effect on your immune system."

Jason's smile brightened when he realized that Alfredo's words were a modified version of the doctor's advice.

"I'm ready for my own surroundings now," Jason said. "The comfort of my bed is much desired."

"Shall I drive you home, my friend?" Alfredo asked, knowing he wasn't about to take no for an answer.

"I'd greatly appreciate that. I'm exhausted and too damned tired to concentrate on driving when all I can see is my pillow. Besides, my car is on the bottom of a pond. I'd like to start leaving that bad memory here with the car I drove myself here in."

"I wasn't about to let you drive. The doctor told me that you already took two potent pills."

"Yep, I should be right by the time I get home," Jason attempted to joke.

THIRTY FOUR

The state prison doctors gave Dakota partial relief from the confining wheelchair. The hard plastic cast was removed from his leg and replaced with an inflatable plastic one. Dakota was thrilled because it granted him access to the showers for the first time since his confinement. On this day, instead of using the allotted time to get fresh air, Dakota limped with a cane to the showers.

Dakota closed his eyes as the hot water massaged his head, ran down his face, seemingly reviving his dirty body. He turned around, opened his eyes just as the lights went out in the shower. It was pitch-black for a second until the light from a tiny window shined upon the darkness. It made the large open shower area a hazy gray. Dakota could see that many men surrounded him. The only exit was blocked; he placed his back against the wall out of the water's stream.

"What the fuck is this?" Dakota asked boldly unafraid.

"Ya know what time it tiz," the smallest of the muscular men spoke. "Tiz time for you to earn yo keep. Ya gonna be my bitch."

"The hell I will," Dakota bellowed. "Get the fuck out of my way before I break your puny neck."

"Ain't no problem, but you gotta suck my dick first," he stated and grabbed himself.

"Get real, fucker. Neither you nor all of your boy toys can make me do that shit. You'd better get more fucking fags," Dakota announced bravely.

Dakota took a step toward the leader, but he vanished behind three muscular mountains. Dakota's upper body remained large and demanding, but the beasts that surrounded him were chiseled freaks of nature. Dakota had little chance of climbing over or breaking through the mountain wall of men before him. Despite the huge disadvantage, Dakota arrogantly charged forward. His first punch flew through the air with deadly force, but landed short of its intended target. He was quickly consumed by the giants around him like a virus on a weakened cell. Dakota hopped on his good leg, fending off the assault with all of his might. An ice pick deflated Dakota's inflatable cast. Instantly, he had trouble bearing weight on the recovering leg.

Dakota's spirit remained high until he was slashed across the stomach with a sharpened piece of metal. The resulting five-inch-long cut was not too deep, but it spewed blood immediately. He grabbed the bleeding area and used the other arm to block the multitude of punches that ambushed him from all sides. Eventually, just like a human stepping on an insect, Dakota was beaten, stomped on and stabbed to near death.

"Girls," the gang leader yelled. "Hol'lup. I gots to get mine." They all backed away and the leader kneeled to the floor. "You gonna give me what I want?" he asked the conquered Dakota.

Dakota's eyes were swollen. His face and body was decorated with too many bruises and cuts to count. He was nearly unconscious and didn't have a sense about him to respond to the gang leader.

"Pick his ass up!" the gang leader demanded.

Several of the monstrosities propped and held Dakota on his bent knees, his head hung low. One of the men grabbed a fistful of hair, pulled Dakota's head back and this opened Dakota's mouth.

"Hol him right der," the gang leader instructed.

He placed a hand in the shower's stream, began massaging himself with the wet hand repeatedly until he obtained an erection. He snapped his fingers, on queue the tip of an ice pick was placed on the side of Dakota's neck. The gang leader inserted his hardened member into Dakota's useless, yet inviting mouth. He pumped his tool against Dakota's dog-like tongue that hung aimlessly out of his mouth.

"Do dat shit!" the gang leader heard.

The simple words ignited a more forceful movement. He held his tool down against Dakota's tongue to generate more friction, then slammed it repeatedly deep into Dakota's throat. He wasn't sure if Dakota was being choked. Realistically, he didn't care. He went about his business until he felt an explosion nearing. Abruptly, he pulled his tool out of Dakota's mouth, finished the climax with his hand, sprayed his juices onto Dakota's face and then rubbed it onto Dakota's face as if he were applying a woman's foundation. The gang leader backed away, removed the remainder of his clothes and bathed in the shower.

One of the muscular beasts lowered to the shower's floor and positioned himself on his hands and knees. The other men moved Dakota's seemingly lifeless body ass up across the back of the makeshift table. Each of the men took turns sodomizing Dakota's rear. When it was all said and done, Dakota was left naked in the shower motionless, yet aware of his ordeal. Sometime later, prison guards found Dakota and rushed him to the prison infirmary.

THE END

EPILOGUE

Several days later, a cell phone belonging to John Jacobs vibrated at his hip. The incoming call was ignored. John simply waited for the final extended vibration to end. This indicated that the caller had left him a voicemail message. He expected to only hear the letters RBR, but the Revenge Beckons Revenge acronym was accompanied with news that Dakota had overdosed with pain medication stolen from the prison infirmary. A great sense of redemption overshadowed the slight guilty feeling.

Jason walked along the water's edge, just short of getting his feet wet in the Virginia Beach sand. He smiled internally, looked across the horizon and threw the prepaid cell phone he'd obtained under a false name into the ocean.

Jason had been a police officer for a long time. Through his detective tenure, coming into contact with shady people was almost a daily occurrence. He learned who to involve and who not to involve when someone wanted to remain anonymous. Jason had sworn that he'd never manipulate the system to this degree, yet the hatred for those related to Monique's murder nearly drove him insane. He indirectly discovered that Dakota was the person behind Monique's murder and had ordered the actions that were taken against him. With this knowledge, wealth and determined revenge, he was led to deceit, fake names and a path of no return.

Damned forever, Jason thought when he realized that his plan had come to fruition and beyond.

He sat in the sand, listened to the tranquil wave sounds crashing against each other. All he thought about was the revenge of Monique's death was like poison. Jason repeated words in his mind until he could recite a poem derived for him.

Poison infiltrates my mind, changing my thoughts. It makes me realize that the pureness which I claim to have, has been diluted. Poison flows from my heart, through my veins, changing my inner being. Poison is making me something I never dreamed I'd be, Darker.

I'm dying...

Poison infiltrates me. Yet, I don't feel weakened. I feel a refreshing change. As one part of me dies, another part is reborn. Changed is what I feel. I welcome this.

Poison, could it be making me better? Does it make me realize what I've always needed?

Poison takes over me. I take over it.

Poison isn't death. Poison is the recognition of my darker side.

AUTHOR BIO

Rique Johnson was born and raised in Portsmouth, Virginia to proud parents Herman and Dorothy Johnson. He finished high school and then joined the U.S. Army six months later because he believed the world had much more to offer than his not-so-fabulous surroundings. After a three-year stint as a soldier, he moved to the Washington, D.C. metropolitan area in 1981 and has made his home in Northern Virginia since 1992.

Rique has always had a passion for the arts. From his desire to be an actor; demonstrated by his role in a homemade "Kung Fu" movie to him writing a monologue to be performed on the original *Star Search*. He trained as a commercial artist and became a proficient photographer in high school. He was a fashion/print model during the first half of the 1980s and has been featured in magazine and newspaper ads for the Hecht Company. He was a local favorite for the fashion designers in the D.C. metro area and has done runway modeling for the Congressional Black Caucus. He was Mr. October in the Black Men of Washington calendar in 1985.

Yet, he has always penciled something. As far as he can remember, his passion for writing started well before his teenage years with love notes to girls that he liked. One of his earliest memories was a love letter he wrote to his fourth-grade teacher. Since that time, he has penciled many songs and various pieces of poetry. He writes things that he simply calls thoughts. Sometimes these thoughts expressed the particular mood he was in and other times they were derived from things that were happening in the world at the time.

His imagination comes across in his novels as creative, bold and sometimes edgy. Rique is often called a storyteller. He writes so that readers can place themselves into the pages of the story and make the pages play like a movie in their own imagination. He is a passionate writer who is unafraid to reveal the sensitivity of a male or himself, thus, evoking an emotional response from the readers.

He lives in Springfield, Virginia.

You may visit the author at www.riquejohnson.com or email him at rique@riquejohnson.com.

EXCERPT FROM

LOVE & JUSTICE

BY RIQUE JOHNSON

AVAILABLE FROM STREBOR BOOKS

CHAPTER 29

Jason is at the hospital bed holding one of Sasha's soft hands between his. His head lays on the bed adjacent to her hip, waiting for any sign of life from her. The door opens and the doctor enters.

"Mr. Jerrard, twenty hours is long enough. She's in a coma and it could be days before she comes out of it. You must go home and get some rest before you are hospitalized for exhaustion. If her condition changes, I'll get in touch with you right away."

The doctor's advice is interrupted by the door opening again as Julie walks in dressed to please as always. Both the doctor's and Jason's eyes focus on her as she steps in.

"Doctor Bodou, this is Julie," Jason states, mentally noting that with this introduction he did not mention ex-wife.

"Pleased to meet you."

"Nice to meet you," Julie greets while sizing up the woman that has taken her place in Jason's heart. "Jason, I tried to reach you at the station today and they told me what happened. How is she, doctor?"

"I was just telling Mr. Jerrard that her vital signs are stable, but at this time she's comatose. There is nothing we can do but wait. I would prefer to have him wait at home...maybe you can help me convince him into going home to get some rest."

"I agree," Julie replies, seizing the moment. "There's nothing more you can do here. You've probably not eaten for hours."

"I know, but I have to be here when she comes out of it."

"If she comes out of it," Dr. Bodou interjects, trying not to sound too pessimistic. "The internal bleeding has stopped. Her condition has stabilized, but, I must caution you, there's a chance that she may never recover," the doctor states, driving the stake farther into Jason's heart.

"I know," Jason concurs in sorrow, "and she is strong. She will recover."

"Jason, let me take you home," Julie suggests. "You can shower. I'll fix you something to eat. You can get some much needed rest. Besides, you can wait at home. There really isn't anything more you can do here. It's in God's hands now."

"Okay," he agrees reluctantly. "Any changes, call me."

"I'll phone you right away, Sir."

As they leave the room, Jason turns and finds it hard to believe that only hours ago, that motionless body lying there was full of life and vigor. What he wouldn't give to have her upset with him. The door closes and the doctor checks her pulse before he leaves.

They arrive at Jason's home with him unusually quiet. His good willful demeanor has conceded to the sorrow his inner being feels. Julie had to drag what little conversation she could out of him on the way over.

"You've made some changes since I was last here," Julie says as she takes a seat in the living room.

"Just a few…would you like a drink?"

"Yes, that would be nice. I think it could help relax me."

"Seven and seven?"

"You remember. I bet you still don't drink and only keep alcohol here for guests."

"I haven't changed much."

"What happened to the divider that was providing closure to the living room?"

"I thought it would match the bedroom furnishings better so I moved it up there."

"Look Jason," Julie says, feeling a need to comfort him. "I know you're very upset about what has happened to Sasha. You're so tense and tight. What you need is one of my famous massages. Do you remember those?"

"Yes, I do."

"Come," Julie instructs. "Sit here."

Jason takes his place between her legs on the floor. Julie administers a squeeze on his tense shoulders. The soft but firm grip sets his mind back to the hours past.

"Maybe if we didn't have that fight," he grieves, "she'd be well now."

"Try not to think about that now and don't go blaming yourself. I'm not trying to sound unconcerned but couples fight every day. We certainly had our share. What makes your fight different from others?"

"There was an attack that followed this one, that's what."

"Yes, if I may steal some of your words, you didn't have control over the attack. You couldn't have possibly known about it. Tell me, why were you two bickering?"

"Do you remember Monique?"

"Oh yes, her," Julie states in a noticeably flatter tone. "She was the one that didn't want you to marry me. I believe she was your first love…"

"Yeah, yeah, yeah, we were only having a simple dinner when Sasha stormed in and…"

"Haven't you learned," interrupting Jason, "we women have a hard time dealing with past associates, friends or otherwise?"

"Can we not talk about this now?"

"Okay, I'm not trying to upset you further. Just sit back, relax and try to clear your mind. This massage should help."

Julie proceeds with the massage, using her fingers on his tense and tight shoulder blades. Jason pushes against her fingers to feel more pressure but Julie's force subsides, bringing his back to the sofa and his head resting on her firm breasts. Julie wraps her arms around his chest giving him a confiding hug.

"Try to relax," Julie suggests. "Worrying will not help anything. God will take care of her."

"You seem to always have the right words at the right time."

She places her hands over each of his ears, tilts his head back and gives him a polite kiss on his forehead. Their eyes lock in a stare, an uncomfortable, passionate stare preventing spoken words. Their minds block out the sounds of the ticking clock on the fireplace mantle and the soothing humming sound of the refrigerator coming from the kitchen, locking them in an unexpected solitude. She kisses him on the tip of his nose, followed by one on the lips. Their eyes lock once more. Slowly, her head falls and their lips meet again, softly. Jason feels his heart pounding, echoing tremors that seem to vibrate through his body. Remembering how soft her lips are, his eyes close, his lips part and they kiss passionately as though they are new-found lovers. The kiss lasts for minutes, only to be broken as Jason turns on his knees. He stands and places her hands into his while dually pulling Julie to her feet. Julie melts to the tender hug that follows.

"You know this shouldn't happen," states Jason, trying to make sense of the situation.

"I know, but why fight the chemistry? A divorce hasn't ended the chemistry—better yet, the passion we've always had between us."

"But?"

"No 'buts.' Look down at your pants. That's real. This passion is real, so why fight it?"

"Julie, Sasha is hospitalized. It just isn't right nor is it the right time. You shouldn't try to use my weakened state to your advantage."

"Lust comes from a weak person. Passion derives from feelings. If she were well and out shopping somewhere, it wouldn't be right when you or I have other people in our lives that we should be committed to. According to some man's rules, you and I making love isn't right; I find that hard to swallow. We have a past. I'm confident that we share feelings for each other to base all of this on, even though you hide yours well. We'll have a future if you let it be. Besides, we make our own rules in life. You of all people should know that. Hell, you taught me this. It's inevitable."

Jason bows his head in a shallow shame. The overwhelming desire to have her again fuels suppressed emotions of his once powerful love for her, igniting a passion that has long passed. "This can't be," faintly splashes through Jason's mind.

"Look at me and tell me this isn't what you want." Jason is unable to utter a single word as she fondles his erect penis. "Furthermore," Julie boasts, "all of this conversation hasn't dampened this guy's spirits."

Jason is first surprised by her actions but recalls that she has always been an aggressive person when it came down to intimacy. Julie tears off the top of his head, breaking the containment of his will. It flows freely to the ceiling, looking down wryly at him giving control to his thought process to his now pulsing penis. She embraces him tenderly, appreciating the comfort of Jason's strong arms around her again. Passion conquers tenderness transforming it into a hard kiss. With no thought of his own, he responds by unbuttoning her silk blouse behind the neck. Halfway through the kiss Julie smiles to herself, realizing that she will finally be enveloped by her beloved Jason. He tackles another button as she releases the button to his pants. Hungrily she takes the zipper down and strokes his warm penis. They kiss as if there were no tomorrow, as if they never divorced, as if they were one again. Jason's pants fall to the floor.

"I'm glad to see that you still don't wear underwear."

Her kiss drops. First, she kisses his neck and lowers to nibble on his erect nipples through his shirt. She lowers more and bites him at the waist. Falling to her knees, she disappears below his waist and his head falls back anticipating the coming pleasure. He closes his eyes and feels his knees weaken to Julie's actions. The sensation has him on the verge of collapsing. He tilts her head back to stop her while he's able to stand.

"Let's continue upstairs," Jason states.

Julie reaches back and throws off her left shoe, then follows with the right.

"Follow me," she says.

Julie starts her stride toward the stairs while simultaneously reaching to the zipper on her skirt, lowering it very slowly while putting an enticing twitch in her walk. In her stride, she pushes her skirt below her hips. It falls to her ankles with her managing to step out of it without losing her pace or losing Jason's attentiveness to her appeal.

Jason is amazed at how seductive Julie continues to be. He steps one foot out of his pants and stumbles as the other is caught in the jumbled mess at his ankle while Julie stops at the staircase motioning him to finish the remaining buttons on her blouse. After releasing the third button she playfully switches from side to side in place.

"Ooh," Julie moans as she ascends the stairs.

Following with anticipation, Jason releases the final buttons with Julie acknowledging the action by drawing her shoulders back, letting the blouse falls to her hands. It is playfully tossed back, landing on his head. As if he needed more seducing, the blouse reaps the scent of his favorite woman's fragrance. Jason fills his lungs capturing its aroma before knocking it from his shoulders to the stairs. Reaching the top of the stairs, Julie turns right, heading for the all-too-familiar bedroom. Following closely behind, Jason turns at the top of the stairs awed by the trail of clothes they've created.

"Jason, Jason," soft and seductively Julie summons.

He follows the voice into the bedroom and closes the door behind him.

Excerpt from

WHISPERS FROM A TROUBLED HEART

By RIQUE JOHNSON

Available from Strebor Books

CHAPTER TWO

A couple of days pass. Jason has hibernated in his home since the funeral. As a result, dishes are piled in the sink and clothes are lying all over the house. This neat, organized person has temporarily abandoned his daily principles and become what many would consider a slob. The only thing he's done constructively, despite medical advice, is work on his body with a weight set in his basement. He has concentrated mostly on his legs and stomach and used lighter weights to tone his damaged chest.

Jason's psyche seems to tell him that his mourning period has ended. There-fore, in an effort to get back to the norm, Jason shaves, showers, and sports one of his finest suits before venturing into the city for a change of scenery. Riding down the main thoroughfare, the growl of his stomach taints the soothing jazz play-ing on the radio.

Not willing to relive the last week or so with his friends at his usual restaurant, he makes an unexpected turn away from breakfast food. He finds himself at the valet parking of La Magnifique, a French restaurant known for its crepes, wines, and other fine authentic foods.

You enter the restaurant through etched glass doors. The walls are painted baby blue with navy blue hand-carved chair railings. The woodwork and window frames are of matching color. A flowery mixture of baby and navy blue along with beige separate the walls from the Cathedral ceiling. The table settings are romantic. A long stick candle with a dim flame burns on each table, not to be overshadowed by the huge crystal chandelier that hangs from the ceiling. Carmen, a charming young woman with dark brown eyes, seats Jason. She has thick black eyebrows and a head of hair of matching color pulled back into a long braid hanging down her back.

"What do you suggest?" asks Jason.

"Depends, what you are in the mood for…seafood?"

"Tempt me."

"The Chef's specialty is a seafood crepe topped with a creamy cheese sauce hiding a hint of burgundy wine."

"That sounds delicious."

"Would you like a cocktail before dinner?"

"Yes, make it leaded."

"Huh?" she says while raising an eyebrow. "Make what leaded?"

"Coffee, caffeinated."

"And the decaffeinated is unleaded?" she asks trying to follow the strange dialog.

"Correct."

"I'll admit that it is an unusual way to refer to coffee," Carmen confesses. "I'll return in a moment."

"Which way is the restroom?"

"Follow me and you will walk right past it."

Jason follows a couple of strides behind her. When he returns to his table, a hot steaming cup of coffee awaits him; its aroma can be enjoyed from a distance. Oddly enough, across from his coffee sits a woman of more than average height on a small frame. Her hair is pinned on top of her head with the front pulled down and teased covering most of her forehead. Her features are strong, a squared chin, high cheekbones, pointy nose and a long neck of tanned color. As Jason gets closer, he notices her most outstanding feature, her seemingly black eyes.

"Excuse me," Jason says, "I've not dined here before so I may have lost my bearings, but, isn't this my coffee?""Yes."

After sitting he asks, "Do you come with the meal?"

"Not exactly…I'll leave if you'd prefer."

"No, you're here now. However, I'm curious as to why?"

"I came in after you, you look gentlemanly and quite frankly, I can use some company."

"Déjà vu, this type of thing seems to follow me where ever I go."

"So, this has happened to you before?"

"Sometime ago."

"Forgive me, I'll leave. Sorry to intrude."

"Your intrusion is welcomed. Even your boldness."

"You like bold women?"

"At times, and you?"

"Bold women do nothing for me," she jokes.

"A sense of humor, good."

"However, bold men ruffle my feathers."

"That can be taken as a positive or negative."

"Positive…definitely positive."

"What's your name?"

"Is that important?"

"It can be, I don't want to be addressing a lunatic."

"You can tell this from a name?"

"Okay, what do you do?"

"Occupation, hmm…next is what do I drive?"

"Are you normally this evasive?"

"Normally, I don't greet men I don't know, besides, those questions aren't necessary. We can enjoy each other's company without the privilege of a history lesson. So," she ponders, "what do we talk about next?"

"Let's talk about that wedding ring you're wearing."

"If it meant anything, I wouldn't be sitting here so pay it no attention."

"It means enough for you to wear it."

"It's all about imagery. On paper, I'm married. My emotions are not. My husband has no time for me."

"I've heard that a time or two."

"You married?"

"Divorced," Jason pauses, "widowed…something like that."

"Which one is it?"

"With the recentness of it, it's too emotional to get into right now."

"Sorry, I'm not trying to pry."

"Don't be, I've recently regained my mental and I would like to keep it that way for a while."

"I've a feeling I'll be divorced soon. I'm not going to put up with his…why are you staring at me?"

Jason says nothing while staring deeply into her dark mysterious eyes, silenced by the ache for passion they reveal.

"Talk to me," she states intrigued by Jason's glaring.

"You're beautiful."

"You're staring at me because you think I'm beautiful?"

"Precisely."

"That's the first compliment I've had in years, too bad it didn't come from my husband."

"Is that any relation to, behind every successful man is a woman, far too often, it isn't his wife?"

"There's a lot of truth to that." She nods. "You're quite handsome yourself."

"Thanks."

"Stop it," she demands, "you're making me nervous."

"I'm just trying to discover the true reason you're sitting here."

"Must there be an ulterior motive?"

"There must be. Simply by the way you're dressed, I can tell that you are no ordinary person."

"How can you be so sure or," she ponders, "are you sure of yourself?"

"Both."

"Is this where you become bold?"

"You call it boldness, I call it being a realist. Before I'd sit here and wonder how it would be to take you to bed, but a few days ago I changed."

"Something to do with being divorced and widowed at the same time?"

"Yes."

"And now?"

"I'm sure you are aware that I've already compromised my position."

"Meaning?"

"By the simple nature of entertaining thoughts of having you physically."

"Surely, you can be more direct," she states, willing to see how far Jason will go.

"Cut to the chase."

"Please."

"Now, I simply ask, would you like to be fucked crazy?"

Her eyes widen as she stumbles for a response, "Is this a question or part of your sentence?"

"You answer that."